MW01533680

I

Chaos

A Dark Romance

J. S. Cannon

Copyright © 2024 J. S. Cannon

All rights reserved

The characters and events portrayed in this book are fictitious. Any
similarity to real persons, living or dead, is coincidental and not intended
by the author.

No part of this book may be reproduced, or stored in a retrieval system,
or transmitted in any form or by any means, electronic, mechanical,
photocopying, recording, or otherwise, without express written
permission of the publisher.

Cover Image: Shutterstock
Cover Design: Canva

Printed in the United States of America

To the women who crave a tall, tattooed protector who will control your body between the sheets and kill anyone who fucks with you in the streets.

It was her chaos that made her beautiful.
ATTICUS

Contents

Trigger and Content Warnings

Death of Family
Depression
References to Suicide
Murder
Stalking
References to Sex Trafficking
Home Invasion
Animal Manipulation (No Abuse)
Dismemberment
Physical Assault
Overdose (Not MC)
Torture
Explicit Sexual Content
Strong Language

Please Read Responsibly.

Blurb

Life was normal until it wasn't.
My family was gone in the blink of an eye, and I
ran.
The tough girl with a chip on her shoulder ran like
a coward.
Ran straight into an existence full of guilt and
despair, hiding for the past two years.
Other than my nine to five, I lock myself in my
apartment, terrified he'll find me and kill me.
I'm alone.
I'm lost.
I'm waiting for it all to end.
By my hand or his.
An innocent question to the stranger next-door
changes everything.
He pushes his way into my life, offering protection
from a past he knows nothing about.
Or so I think.
A split-second decision changes my life in ways I
never imagined.
Death brings life and it changes me forever.
Secrets are revealed and everything unravels.
I'm not alone like I thought.
I'm not as hidden as I hoped.
The man who ripped my life apart has only one
obsession.

To see me dead.

While "Chaos" is a standalone dark romance, you will see characters from "Rage".
It's not necessary to read "Rage" before reading "Chaos", but it is highly recommended.

Prologue

Savannah

My body jolts as an agonizing scream pierces my ears.

Mom.

Shooting up in bed, my eyes dart around the room, disoriented.

A thud fills the room as something hard slams into the wall down the hall.

My heart beats erratically, my stomach churning with every worst-case scenario possible. My body doesn't want to move, but my mind screams to get to my mother.

Forcing myself from the bed, I tip toe across the room as quietly as I can. Approaching the door, I turn the knob, gritting my teeth as it makes a clicking sound. Taking a deep breath, I pull open the door, peeking through the threshold.

Glancing to my left, there's nothing out of place. Just then, my father's cries reach me and my eyes dart to the right.

My world comes to a screeching halt.

My parents' bedroom door is open and lying in the doorway on the floor is my mother. Her body is twisted at an odd angle, like she was thrown across the room. My feet move involuntarily, desperate to help her.

As I creep down the hall, I trip over something, bracing against my brother's doorframe to stop myself from falling. Peering down, Dylan is lying on his stomach, blood oozing from the back of his head.

A scream rises in my throat, but I swallow it down at the sound of my father's wailing. He's on his knees, and when I focus on his face, he's jerking his head to the side frantically.

Run.

Shaking my head violently, I try to convey to him that I won't leave my family. His expression is pleading as I silently move closer, catching a glimpse of the large barrel resting against his temple.

"We could have avoided this if you would have given me what I wanted."

My blood runs cold as I recognize *his* voice.

"Your wife is dead. Your son is dead. You're next and then your beautiful daughter."

My uncle.

My eyes find my mother again, my chest caving in at her blank, lifeless stare.

This has to be a nightmare.

Wake the fuck up!

My gaze collides with my father's for only a moment before the gun goes off, the sound making my ears ring. His head jerks to the side awkwardly before his body falls to the floor.

Both my hands fly to my mouth, doing little to muffle the scream ripped from my throat. A large figure comes into view, and I can barely make out who it is through my blurry vision.

Colin, my father's brother.

Two men file in behind him and their gazes lock onto me.

"Savannah, dear. I know you're upset but come here to me and I can explain everything."

His casual tone makes my stomach turn. "You just killed my fucking family!"

"Yes, but I can tell you why and we can move past this." His empty eyes meet mine and I'm terrified.

He said I'm next.

The will to live has never been stronger than it is at this moment.

My chaotic mind has always teetered on the edge, questioning if this life is really worth it.

Now, as I look at the man who just ripped my world apart, I'm sure I don't want to die by his hand. "Fuck you, murderer! I won't be your victim." Spinning on my heels, I take off running down the hall.

"Get her!" Colin yells to his henchmen.

Reaching the staircase, I run down the stairs as fast as my legs will take me, gripping the banister to stop myself from falling. My momentum has me slamming into the front door, but I recover quickly, gripping the knob in my hand.

It won't budge.

Checking the deadbolt and the knob, they're unlocked. My mind races as I realize they somehow locked it from the outside.

I don't have time for this shit if I want to live. I glance behind me; Colin's men are halfway down the stairs.

In a split-second decision, I pick up the chair where my father always sits to take off his boots when he gets home. With all my strength, I throw it into the wall length window next to the front door. Glass shatters everywhere, but I don't hesitate. Jumping through the window, I grit my teeth as glass punctures the soles of my feet through my socks.

The men yell curses behind me, but I don't stop.

Heading for the woods across the street, I know it's the only chance I have. It's dense and easy to hide amongst the huge trees and thick brush. Dylan and I used to camp here all the time before I started college.

The thought of my brother constricts my chest, and I push all thoughts of my family out of my mind.

I have to stay focused.

I'm running for my fucking life.

Chapter One

Savannah

Have you ever met someone who doesn't want to live most days, but still fights tooth and nail to hang on?

That's me.

I'm that person.

Depression is a fickle bitch.

While I've fought so hard the past two years to stay hidden and survive, I often wonder why I bother.

There's nothing left for me here.

I'm alone.

Plagued with memories of a family that was murdered over my father's stupid fucking business.

His own brother shot him without a second thought. That was after he killed my mother and brother.

Whoever said time heals all is full of shit. My wounds have only festered until it's consumed me completely.

I've been spiraling since that night. Every day is harder than the last, harder to find the will to go on.

What would happen if my car just veered off the road and ran into a tree?

Would I see my family again if I took the entire

bottle of sleeping pills instead of just two?

A gunshot to the head would be painless, right?

I've always had dark thoughts.

Maybe some wires got crossed in my brain when I came out of my mother. Maybe it's hereditary. I always heard whispers about my grandmother having mental issues. She was a bitter old woman who thought pitting family members against each other would have us all turning to her.

She was wrong. She thought her hateful words were showing us love in some fucked up way. Most of us grew to resent her and eventually cut off all contact.

I think about her often lately. Is this how she felt? Lonely and depressed?

Alone.

I was never the one to have a lot of friends.

I usually only had one at a time until they betrayed me in some way. Always talking shit behind my back. As I grew older, my hurt feelings morphed into anger. Anyone who started shit with me found themselves on the other side of my fists.

My parents didn't understand me either, but they never turned their back on me. My mother hated the fighting, but my father taught me how to fight harder. He told me to never take any shit, but she told me to pick my battles.

They were the only people who truly loved me. And my little brother, of course.

Dylan.

He was only fourteen when he was murdered.

He was your typical, moody teenage boy, but he was a teddy bear to me. We had our stupid little fights, but we didn't stay mad long and I'm the only one who ever got an apology out of him.

Honestly, I recognized myself in him. We shared the same darkness. I think that's why we were so close given our age difference. The five-year age gap between us should have made us enemies, like most siblings, but we were unique.

He played his video games and blared his music, but he was mature for his age. He was a loner like me, and it helped us understand each other better.

It made us friends.

I was still living at home when I turned nineteen. It was early fall, and I was preparing for my second year at college. Dad said I could go anywhere I wanted; he only wanted the best for me. The thought of leaving my family broke my heart, so I chose to attend a university close to home. The commute wasn't bad, about forty-five minutes.

Everything was set, only a few days before I'd continue my journey into business management.

That night, my world changed forever.

My life shattered into a million pieces, never to be whole again.

He murdered my entire family.

My father's brother.

My uncle.

Everyone died that night except me.

The only reason I didn't is because I heard my mother's screams.

Dad always said if anything ever happened to run for my life and never look back.

And that's exactly what I did.

I never returned to school.

I lost my parents.

My younger brother.

The evil son-of-a-bitch took everything from me, and I ran.

I'm filled with grief and guilt. Why didn't I stay and fight? I had no problem fighting anyone else, but I couldn't fight the man who killed my family.

Some days I wish I would've stayed and let him kill me, too. At least I wouldn't have to live with this hole in my chest, the pain of the memories. Other days, I want to find the motherfucker and torture him slowly.

It's a toss-up at this point to see which emotion will win.

I may drown in despair and walk through this world like a ghost.

Or, maybe one day, I'll find my balls and track him down.

Either way, I'm not the person I was two years ago.

Savannah Banks is dead.

She's been replaced by Sav Callahan, courtesy of Nick West, who I met a few months after leaving home.

I was trying to get a job at a local diner to make some cash.

After I ran away that night, I never stopped except to sleep at shelters. I was exhausted from all the walking, but I lucked out a few times, people I ran across offering me a ride.

I was staying in a women's shelter across the state, hours from home, lost and traumatized. I woke up one day and realized I needed to pull myself together and try to move on, or at least house and feed myself.

Lying to the owner of the local diner, I told him my home caught fire and I had no identification. He wasn't having any of it and I left defeated, with no idea what to do.

As I was walking down the sidewalk, headed back to the shelter, a guy yelled at me. "Hey!"

Quickening my pace, he still caught up to me. "Wait. I'm not going to hurt you. I want to help."

"Why?" I blurted out. It probably sounded shitty, but if there's one thing I've learned, everyone has an agenda.

He smiled sadly. "Your story sounded like bullshit from a mile away, that's why he turned you down. You can go to the courthouse and get copies of your identification, but obviously you don't want to. So, I'm going to say you're running from something."

My mouth opens to speak, but my throat is suddenly dry, scared this is some kind of trap. My eyes dart around, inspecting my surroundings, waiting for Colin to materialize, and put a bullet between my eyes.

He must sense my fear as he continues. "It's okay, I promise. It's not my business why you're running, but I'm willing to help you get a new id."

I fight like hell to hold back the tears and swallow thickly at the burn in my throat. "Why would you help me?"

He takes a step forward, understanding in his eyes. "I know what it's like to disappear. I can get you the documents you need to get a job and whatever else you may need."

Eyeing him cautiously, I'm waiting for the punchline, wondering what he will want from me. "I don't have any money."

He gives me a lopsided grin. "Well, I can't get you any of that."

My lips tug up just a fraction and it's a foreign feeling. I can't remember the last time I even thought about smiling. "How will I pay you then?"

"You won't. I'll get you what you need, no strings attached. Call it my good deed for the week." He grins. "My name is Nick by the way. What's yours?"

He watches me expectantly as I think of a name on the spot. I don't want to lose my identity completely. I need to keep a piece of myself and my family. The nickname my dad always called me comes to mind and it is a version of the truth. "Sav."

He nods thoughtfully. "Sav what?"

Exhaling deeply, I wasn't prepared for this today. I give him the first last name I think of. "Callahan."

"Nice to meet you, Sav Callahan. I'm Nick West. Come with me."

I followed him back to the diner, and he bought me lunch. We talked for hours, and I grew to like him.

He never asked what happened to me and I never asked him about his past. There was an unspoken bond between us that afternoon and I was grateful for it.

After lunch, I went back to the shelter, but Nick came by later that afternoon. He didn't ask me to come to his place and I was thankful for it. Even though I appreciate his help and company, there was no way in hell I was going to a stranger's house.

He brought his laptop and a small id printer, taking my picture and making it all right in front of me. He said he would work on a birth certificate and social security card at home and bring it to me the next day.

And he did.

Then, he came back the day after that.

Before I knew it, he was coming over a few nights a week. We'd watch tv or play cards, anything to block out the noise of our past.

He became my friend.

He helped me get a job at the diner and within a month, I had enough saved to rent a little apartment. It was nothing special, but it was mine.

He showed up one night, disoriented and talking out of his head. He confided in me that his past haunts him every day. I didn't pry, instead letting him tell me his secrets at his own pace.

He was a recovering drug addict. Heroin was his crutch.

To say I was stunned is an understatement. I listened without judgement as he told me how he got mixed up with the wrong men and owed them a lot of money.

Nick was supposed to sell the drugs, not use them. His family and friends had severed all contact with him, so he had no one to turn to. A problem he created, but sad, nonetheless.

When he couldn't come up with the money, they shot up his house in the middle of the night. His girlfriend was killed in their bed.

By the way he was talking, I could tell a part of him died that night too.

Through his grief, he made the decision to get clean. He said it was hell, but being off the drugs gave him clarity and helped him work through his guilt.

After he finished his story, the more he talked, the more I realized he was high. My heart sank as I watched him scratch his arms and ramble on to the point where he wasn't making any sense.

I didn't call him out on it for fear he may leave, and something happen to him. I thought I was being a good friend, asking him to stay, offering my worn couch as a bed. He squeezed my hand tightly, thanking me for being such a good listener and friend.

He left despite my objections.

I couldn't sleep for worrying about him.

The next morning, I turned on the local news to see his face. He was found on the front steps of his house.

He overdosed.

My heart was broken, imagining him dying, alone and scared, outside in the middle of the night.

I couldn't save him.

Just like I couldn't save my family.

He's been gone for over a year and a half and I still miss him.

Why does everyone I care about always die?

Chapter Two

Declan

She gets out of her car, completely exhausted.

I'm surprised the old beater gets her back and forth to the hole-in-the-wall diner where she works. I've stopped by the place a few times, and Savannah Banks works her ass off.

I plan my evenings around her work schedule, making sure I'm available when she gets home. She's set in a routine, checking her mailbox before she goes inside, locking herself away for the night.

The girl never goes anywhere.

She's barely making ends meet with her job, just one of the many reasons why she lives here. This apartment building is older, and no one does maintenance. I hate living here, but I won't leave her to fend for herself, even if she doesn't know I exist.

Locking the front door behind me, I head down to the mailboxes, pacing myself so we get there at the same time. As usual, she doesn't notice me, which allows me the time to take her in.

She's a gorgeous girl, but her pain creates a heavy tension around her, and it pulls at something in my chest.

She's slender, with curves in all the right places. Long chocolate hair flows down her back with a crease through the middle from having it in a ponytail at work. Her smooth, pale skin looks fragile like a porcelain doll. I can't see them now, but I know her green eyes are dull and lifeless like every time I've seen them before.

Being this close, pretending I don't see her is difficult. Her sadness is so thick I can taste it like a stagnant paste on my tongue. The bitter flavor sends a shudder through my body. I've never been an empathetic person, but this girl's emotions have my own screaming to fucking fight.

Opening my box, I pull out the junk mail, sifting through it to buy me a few more moments in her space.

She closes her mailbox, turning the key to lock it. She turns to walk to her door, and I head towards mine, strategically across the breezeway from her apartment.

"Excuse me?" She speaks as I twist the doorknob.

There's a second of shock that rolls through me before I turn around. "Yeah?"

"What's your name?" She tilts her head to the side, studying me.

Clearing my throat, I respond casually. "Declan, but everyone calls me Dex."

She looks at the mail in her hand, pulling an envelope from the top of the stack. "Declan Archer?"

Swallowing thickly, hearing her say my name in that sweet voice does something to me. "That's me." I smile, but she doesn't return the sentiment.

"This was put in my box by mistake." She holds

the envelope between us, and I gently take it from her.

"Sorry about that." I say, glancing at the mail.

It's junk, the same shit I get every day. My boss, Jase, has it delivered so I look like a normal tenant while I'm here. How the hell he got in her box, I don't know, but I'm not surprised.

"No problem." She nods curtly, turning back to her front door.

"Hey, what's your name?" I know her damn name, but I don't want this interaction to end. She has me intrigued and I want more.

"Oh, um, Sav." She nods again and hurries inside her apartment.

I already knew she's been using an alias, and I don't blame her. It would've done her better to choose something further away from her real name, but I don't hold it against her. She needs something from her old life to ground her, and I understand that.

Heading inside, I toss the mail on the counter and pull out my phone. Finding my chat with Jase, I text him.

Me: Why did you put my fake mail in her mailbox?

Jase: Did she talk to you?

Me: Yes, asshole. She talked to me.

Jase: You're welcome. I should've done it months ago.

Me: Prick. Leave the girl alone. She's been

through enough. I don't need her to talk to me in order to protect her.

Jase: But you *want* her to.
Me: IF she WANTS to.
Jase: Pussy!
Me: Shut the fuck up.
Jase: Your gratitude humbles me.

I flip him off with an emoji and he sends back the laughing face.

Jackass.

We've talked about Savannah every day and Jase has it in his head that I need to push things along with her. He thinks because he stalked his wife into loving him that it will work for everyone. Where Savannah is concerned, pushing her may make things worse.

I'll be the nice guy and earn her trust.

It can't be *that* hard.

Fuck.

Making my way to the bedroom, I sit on the edge of my bed. Blowing out a breath, I run my fingers through my hair, unsure what to do next. We only shared a few words, but it was enough to draw me in.

Glancing at the bulletin board hanging on the wall, my eyes search her face in every picture pinned to it. She's lost in her head in every photo, only existing in this life to work and pay bills.

A part of me wants her happiness, but a larger part of me is drawn to her sadness.

How does a person come back from all she's lost? How is she supposed to enjoy life while she's being hunted?

Savannah knows she's the prey, but I don't think she realizes just how close the predator is.

Chapter Three

Savannah

There were a few boys who caught my attention in high school, but I never had a boyfriend. Between fighting and trying to keep my grades up, I never pursued any of them.

I saw a lot of pretty boys in my first and only year at college, but I still focused on my grades and finding my own way at a new school. Starting a new and *calmer* chapter in my life, I sidelined any attempts at getting to know the other students.

Talking to Declan Archer when I got home today was not on my agenda. I could've waited until he went inside and slid the mail under his door.

That's *exactly* what I should've done.

I've noticed him as we usually check our mail around the same time every day. He's lived here for a few months, but we've never spoken.

When I made the decision to be neighborly and give him his mail, I wasn't prepared.

It's the first time I've taken a good look at him.

He's fucking gorgeous.

He's tall, at least six foot two with a muscular build that most men work their entire lives for. Black and gray ink covers every inch of his visible skin, like the magnificent canvas he is. His face is perfection with a strong jaw line peppered with a few days of stubble. He may be eye candy, but his piercing blue eyes caught me off guard.

They were kind.

It's odd to look that deeply into his physical attributes, but he gives off protective vibes.

Those high school boys may have caught my attention before, but no one has ever thrown me for a loop like this man.

It's a *bad* idea to get close to anyone.

Danger lurks around every corner, and I refuse to drag anyone into this shit show with me.

Nick was the exception.

He came into my life offering help with no strings attached.

A friend.

In the end, the drugs were stronger than our friendship. The drugs he hid so well until the last night I saw him.

When I lost him, I told myself I wouldn't open up to anyone else. I don't know what I did in my past life to deserve all this death and heartbreak, but I can't let it happen again.

Even if I spend the rest of my life alone.

It was hard getting out of bed this morning.

My head is killing me and my muscles ache. I'm too damn young to feel this old.

I'm always exhausted, rather it be mentally or physically.

Or both.

The diner isn't a bad place to work. I'm grateful for the job. It kills my feet and I'm running around non-stop to keep the customers happy, but it's not the most horrible thing in the world. It doesn't pay much, but I'm getting by. I was able to get the job, thanks to Nick and the counterfeit documents.

Honestly, I'm scared to push my luck in finding anything that pays better. What if someone can tell my id is fake? What if my uncle finds me?

It's better to stay where I am. I doubt Colin would ever set foot in a place like the diner. He would find it beneath him.

Glancing at the clock, it's almost five and I couldn't be more ready to clock out and go home. The lunch rush almost killed me, and I had a few customers who were pissed because we ran out of mayo and pickles.

Keeping a practiced smile on my face, I apologized to them all, but some still made a fuss. One lady made a scene and my dormant temper flared. "Do you want me to bring you a cucumber? Your sour attitude would turn it into a pickle in no time."

A throat cleared behind me and I closed my eyes. I knew that sound and my stomach sank, betting Clive was about to give me the pink slip.

Opening my eyes, I slowly turned around and sure enough, my boss was staring at me with an unreadable expression. "Go to my office."

I did as I was told and five minutes later, the door opened, and Clive strolled in.

"Clive, I'm sorry. I-"

He raised his hand to silence me as a grin

tugged at his lips. "You're a fiery one, little Sav."

My eyes widened, confused, and momentarily stunned. Clive never smiles.

He took a seat behind his desk and continued. "Stop looking at me like that. I'm not going to fire you. That old hag is always bitching about something."

My body sagged at his words, and he grinned again. "You're an open book. People can see every emotion play across your face."

That is one-hundred percent true. My parents always told me I could never hide my emotions.

"I'm still sorry. This is your business, and I shouldn't have spoken to her like that."

"It's okay, Sav. Just try to keep it reeled in next time?" He lifted an eyebrow in question, and I nodded.

"I promise."

I've peopled enough today. I need to be in my own space and left alone.

Ironic for someone who is lonely as hell.

There's a difference between being surrounded by strangers and being in the company of someone you care about.

The clock on the wall strikes five and I head to the back to grab my purse. Swinging by the timeclock, I punch out quickly and head out to my car.

Poor Bessy has seen better days, but she gets me from point a to point b. That's all I can ask for at this point. She finally cranks on the third try and

I lay my head on the steering wheel while gripping it with both hands.

I'm still breathing.

That's all that matters.

At least that's what I tell myself.

Chapter Four

Declan

Savannah pulls up and her exhaustion is obvious as she walks down the breezeway to the mailboxes.

I'm careful to make myself known, clearing my throat as I come up beside her. "Hey, Sav."

She startles, her head jerking towards me before she replies. "Oh. Hey, Declan."

She goes back to what she's doing and I'm standing here like an idiot, trying to think of something else to say.

I fucking kill people for a living, but I can't carry on a conversation with this girl.

My eyes roam her body, and I find myself getting agitated because she looks thinner. I don't know if it's from all the stress or the diner doesn't pay her enough to buy groceries.

There's no one to look after her.

I'll remedy that. "Have you eaten?"

She slowly slides her gaze to me. "What?"

"I made dinner-"

She cuts me off. "No, thank you. I already have something made."

My jaw clenches as she brushes me off. "I'll make you a plate and bring it over."

"I said 'no thank you', Declan." She rushes out, and I take a step back.

Raising my hands in surrender, I may have lost

this round, but lucky for her, I like a challenge.

She spares me an unreadable glance before walking away, disappearing into her apartment.

Savannah is burying herself under my skin and it's fucking with my head.

The agony in her eyes is as sweet as the finest Moscato.

The aura of loneliness surrounding her calls to my withered soul.

The depression in her mind makes me want to nurture her like a wounded animal.

I don't know what she's doing to me. I feel like she's a reflection of myself, filled with pain and horrific memories.

I've gotten nothing for months except stolen glances. Now that we've spoken, I feel closer to her, even as she rejects me.

Entering my apartment, I head to the kitchen, piling the ingredients I'll need on the counter. Pulling out a skillet, I begin cooking steak with peppers and rice.

I don't have a clue if she'll like it or not, but it's 'real food' and she needs nutrients. She's sunk too far into her depression to properly take care of herself. I won't stand by and watch her wither away any longer.

Reaching into the cabinet, I pull out a tupperware container, filling it to the brim with hearty food. Opening the fridge, I grab two beers.

Slipping out of the front door, I place the bowl and beers just far enough back from her apartment she'll be able to see them through the peephole. Knocking three times, I rush inside my unit, closing the door quickly.

Looking through my own peephole, I wait to see if she'll take the dinner. A few beats pass and just when I think she won't open the door, it creaks open slowly.

She stares at the food for a moment like it may bite her. She glances at my door, and I don't blink, taking in every inch of her dark beauty. Something flashes in her eyes before she bends down, picking up the bowl and beers.

She looks at my door one last time before heading back inside and I grin.

I wish I could watch her as the dinner I made touches her lips.

Will her eyes close as the flavors bursts across her tongue?

Will she gag at the taste of it because she doesn't like peppers?

I'd like to see both reactions, but for a completely different reason.

Get a fucking grip, man.

Stepping away from the door, I head to the kitchen to make my plate. I eat quickly, knowing I need to dive into work.

Maybe it will get her off my mind for a while…

The rest of the night trickles by, uneventful.

Everything is quiet in Savannah's apartment, as usual.

The room is dark as I sit on the couch, my laptop propped on my thighs. Jase sent some files over for me to review, no new information piquing my interest.

CCTV footage comes up empty, but I request it be sent anyway.

Photos of safe houses that aren't currently occupied, but I want to see for myself.

Even if the information is the same as yesterday and a complete waste of my time, I still comb through it relentlessly.

I have to.

For her.

After spending a few hours staring at the laptop screen, my eyes blur and I power it off. Laying it on the coffee table, I stand up, stretching my arms above my head as I walk to the window, scanning the breezeway and the parking lot.

Everything is quiet.

Heading towards my bedroom, I shed my clothes, sliding between the cool sheets. My eyes close and I see Savannah, pain and torment dulling the brightness inside her.

I don't know how yet, but I'll break her.

I will fucking break her over and over until her fire explodes from every crack I create.

Chapter Five

Savannah

I'm driving home from work when an unwanted thought pops into my head.

Will Declan be there when I get home?

I felt like a jerk cutting him off yesterday, but I couldn't help it. I'm the picture of an introvert, a damn recluse if I'm being honest.

He was being nice.

He left me a bowl of the most delicious steak and peppers I've ever tasted and a couple of beers.

The little bit of food in my apartment is bullshit junk, but it's all I can afford. Pasta and rice are what I mostly survive on, adding a little meat in the mix if I have a good day making tips.

Dinner hit the spot and the beers helped me relax. I slept more peacefully than I have in two years.

Declan is a good guy, but I can't let him close.

I try to stay away from people. It only hurts when you let them in. I took a chance when Nick and I became friends and look what happened.

I can't lose anyone else.

My family is gone, and friends are off the table too. I'm trying my best to move on with my life, even though I'm stuck in the same cycle every day. All I can hope for is one day, my heart will stop hurting and my mind will fall silent.

Pulling into the parking lot, I shut off my old

car, heading towards the building.

Like clockwork, Declan steps outside, closing his door behind him.

My stomach flutters at the sight of him and I shut that shit down.

Or so I thought.

He walks past me without saying a word and I'm bothered by it. "Hey, Declan." I murmur, opening my box.

"Hey." He mumbles and my stomach twists with nerves.

Why does he have this effect on me? It's better if we keep our distance. He will stay out of danger.

But my mouth doesn't stop. "How was your day?"

His head snaps up, his eyes colliding with mine. I'm taken aback by the intensity I see in them before they soften a moment later. "They didn't work you too hard at the diner, did they?"

My eyes widen. "How do you know I work at the diner?"

He chuckles and it lights up his entire face. "It's one of three restaurants in this town. I've eaten there a time or two."

For the first time in a long time, I smile. "True."

His grin fades as he takes a step closer. "You have a beautiful smile."

Dipping my head, embarrassment heats my face.

"Don't hide from me." His fingers twitch like he wants to touch me, but he holds himself back.

Thank God.

I can't handle a compliment, much less his touch.

It's been so long since I've felt any kind of affection. Two years since I've had someone hug me or kiss me on the cheek.

Fuck.

Who was it? Mom or Dad?

I can't fucking remember.

It's made me bitter in some ways. I've come to hate the idea of something I crave more than anything.

"Sav." My name on his lips pulls me from my thoughts and I quickly lock my box, spinning towards my apartment.

As I slide my key into the lock, a large hand wraps around my wrist. "Hey."

My body stills as I soak in the warmth of his skin against mine. It feels so strange yet comforting.

Tears threaten to fall as I glance up at him.

He looks worried, but I can't give him reassurance when I'm about to fall apart. Shaking my head, I dart inside, closing the door in his face.

Hurrying to my bedroom, I shut the door, sliding down slowly until my ass hits the floor. Wrapping my arms around my knees, I let the tears fall, sobbing quietly.

I'm so fucked up.

This hollow void inside me is too much most days.

It would be so easy to give up.

Easy to let go so I wouldn't have to feel this shit anymore.

No matter what happens in my life, it always leads back to them.

My guilt.

My anger.

My dead family.

A hot shower didn't help my mood.

I decided once again to stay in the land of the living, but it all still seems like a waste. I have no one and I work at a diner to pay for a shitty apartment just to get up every day and do it all over again.

I'm merely existing and I don't see any glimmer of hope in my future.

Will it always be like this? Running and starting over to keep from dying?

I'm so fucking tired.

Twenty-one years on this earth and the last two have felt like multiple lifetimes, filled with nothing but pain and solitary confinement. I could try to meet people and make friends, but I'm terrified if my uncle ever finds me, he will kill everyone I care about.

He did it before.

As I lay my hairbrush on the counter, there's a knock on my door.

My body tenses.

Is it Colin?

Has he finally found me?

Grabbing the baseball bat from the side of my bed, I tiptoe through the apartment, quietly approaching the door. Looking through the peephole, I'm stunned and relieved to see Declan on the other side.

He knocks again and I decide to walk away. There's no reason to talk to him more than necessary. It was a mistake trying to start a conversation with him earlier and he probably thinks I'm batshit crazy after my reaction.

He knocks a third time. My mind screams for my legs to keep moving, but my body doesn't obey. Before I know what's happening, I disable the alarm, unlock the deadbolt, then the doorknob. There's a high-pitched whine as I open the door slowly.

He stands there, his shoulders slumped forward, his hands propped on each side of the door frame. He slowly lifts his head, his blue eyes boring into mine. "Can I come in?"

Before I can respond, he quickly steps through the threshold, closing the door behind him. He eyes me for a moment before locking it, his gaze darting to the baseball bat in my hand.

"You don't need that, little one. I'm not going to hurt you." He speaks softly and the anxiety churning in my stomach eases a fraction.

"What do you want?" I ask, the bat still firmly in my grip.

He turns his head from side to side slowly,

taking in my apartment. He notices the alarm on the wall, my shitty furniture and finally his gaze settles on me once again. "We need to talk."

For a moment, I debate telling him to leave, but for some reason, I want to hear what he has to say. Taking a few steps backwards, I sit in the chair, motioning for him to sit on the couch.

He nods, taking a seat on the cushion closest to me. "I want you to hear me out."

That's not a good sign.

Sitting back in the chair, I lay the bat across my lap, nodding for him to continue.

"Your fucking tears sliced me open, and I haven't been able to think about anything else. It's so obvious, Sav. I see every bit of pain in your eyes. Your past is crippling you. You need someone in your life to talk to."

Tears prick my eyes, and my instinct is to recoil from his words, the truth shredding my chest with unbearable agony. I drop my head, gripping the bat with both hands, needing something to hold onto. I can't even conjure the energy to tell him to get out. I'm paralyzed by my emotions, the instability too much to bear.

There's shuffling sounds in the distance and then Declan is before me on his knees. He lifts my chin with his finger, and the surprising move forces me to open my eyes. With blurry vision, I still don't miss the concern etched across his face.

"Tell me how to help you, little chaos? There's so much going on in that pretty little head of yours."

I slowly find my voice through the lump in my throat. "I had someone to talk to and now he's dead. Everyone I care about dies. You can't help me, Declan. I can't talk about it."

He nods slowly, his warm finger still holding my chin. "Your past is your own, but you can't go on like this." He cups my cheek in his palm. "I'll be your life vest when it tries to drown you."

Between his intense gaze and his warm touch, I can't deny I want him here. I don't have an explanation for what I'm feeling, but it's nice to have someone with me. "Do you want to watch tv?"

He gets to his feet, holding out his hand to me. Leaning the bat against the wall, I take his hand hesitantly. He pulls me from the chair, and I sigh with relief when the tears fade.

"Do you want something to snack on?" He asks, heading into the kitchen.

This is fucking embarrassing.

There's only instant noodles and microwave dinners. "You won't find anything in there."

I turn my head to find his expression dark, but when he catches me looking, his eyes soften. "I'll be right back."

He darts out the door and I jump off the couch to lock it. I have a compulsive need to keep my door locked at all times. He probably isn't coming back anyway.

I'm fucked up.

I'm a sad, pathetic girl who doesn't know how to move on with her life.

I'm either depressed or angry as hell.

I want to stay in bed all day or find Colin and kill him before he can kill me.

My mind plays one extreme or the other.

There's no peace.

A knock on my door snaps me back to the present and I realize my hand is still on the knob. Looking through the peephole, all my dark thoughts scatter as I see Declan waiting on the other side. Opening the door quickly, he saunters inside, one arm full of boxes and bags.

"What is all that?" I ask, locking the door again.

He deposits the load on the kitchen counter, and my lips twitch as half of it hits the floor. He curses, bending over to pick it up.

His dark jeans pull tightly against his ass, and I find myself enjoying the view. Until he straightens and turns towards me, catching me in the act.

My cheeks heat as he gives me a knowing smirk. "I don't know what you like, so I grabbed everything with sugar in it."

My chest vibrates with a feeling I haven't felt in so long.

Laughter.

I actually laugh.

It shocks me to my core and when I meet Declan's gaze, his lip's part, his eyes locked onto my mouth.

My face burns with embarrassment. It's

ridiculous that something so trivial affects me so deeply.

He steps forward, gripping my hand. "I need you to do that more."

I gasp at the contact, and before I can take a step back, he grips the back of my neck, crushing our mouths together.

I'm frozen for what feels like forever, but his teasing lips melt away my doubts.

His tongue traces the seam of my lips and I open for him, my head spinning from the sudden turn of events. My hands slide up his torso and I feel the ridges of muscle through his shirt. My fingers come to rest on his chest, curling into the fabric. He pins me against him with one hand around my waist, the other fisting my long hair.

It would be so easy to get lost in this man, but I can't.

I'm too far gone in my own bullshit to bring him down with me. I'm a fucking basket case, not knowing how I'll feel from one minute to the next.

Pushing at his chest, he lets go immediately, his eyes filled with concern.

"I can't do this." Stepping away from him, I go to the door and open it. "I need some time alone."

He watches me for a few moments before running his fingers through his dark hair. He heads towards the door, stopping when he's in front of me. "You know where I am."

As he closes the door behind him, confusion and heartache settle in my chest.

Is this what life has in store for me?

Losing everyone I love has scarred me and I won't let anyone else close.

Staring at the floor where Declan stood when he kissed me, the sadness suffocates me.

The walls are closing in.

Scrunching up the fabric of my shirt, I bring it to my face, inhaling deeply.

I still smell him.

Still feel his hands on me.

Still taste him.

Rushing to my bedroom, I change clothes and throw my hair into a ponytail.

I can't handle this shit.

I have to get out of here.

Chapter Six

Declan

She's fractured and a compliment sent her spiraling.

I took a chance, pushing myself into her apartment, showing her a glimpse of the real me.

Patience isn't my strong suit.

I couldn't take the tears in her eyes. It felt like a dagger through my fucking heart.

I couldn't stay away from her.

She's a beautiful fucking disaster.

Chaos in her mind.

Pain in her heart.

Emptiness in her soul.

Everything about Savannah calls to me and I know I'm fucked. She has no clue who I really am. Even if she did, she'd push me away further because of all the secrets and my past.

She'd realize what kind of man I am and how the version she's seen so far is a façade.

I'd lose her and that thought alone makes me fucking sick.

I'm becoming obsessed with her. Or I'm in denial and I've been obsessed since the moment I saw her beautiful ass step out of her death trap car.

Something locked into place when she laughed.

The world stood still, and nothing existed except for Savannah. Her tragic features morphed into stunning beauty in those few moments, and it took my damn breath.

She's starved for affection, being alone too long.

She's gorgeous and could have any man she wants. I see the way those pricks stare at her while she's working at the diner.

I was honest when I told her I've eaten there a time or two, but I can't count how many times I've sat in my truck across the street and watched her. I needed to know she's safe. Not only from her uncle, but from the slimy pricks that salivate at her every move while she serves them.

I'm the only one she's given her attention to, and I know she feels the tension brewing between us.

Based on that assumption and the overwhelming need to, I kissed her.

Fuck.

She ruined me when her hot little tongue met mine and the rest of the world disappeared.

For a moment.

She got lost in her head and before I knew what was happening, she pushed me away.

I've never met anyone so terrified of getting close to someone.

She'd mentioned having a friend before that died.

Him.

Once I realized she was talking about Nick West, my jealousy subsided. I discovered him while digging around, researching how she got the fake identification documents. It's sad what happened to the kid, and I'll always be grateful he was there to help her when she needed it the most.

She's lost everything and she's skittish about letting me in, but I'm not giving up. After tasting her, I'm hellbent on making her mine and giving her the safety she needs.

She may be battling some strong ass demons, but I have my own as well.

Our fucked-up emotions could only lead to a toxic and exhausting rollercoaster, but damn do I want it.

She's broken and I want to be sliced open by every jagged edge of her shattered pieces.

I want to absorb all her pain and savor the downward spiral she's been trapped in for so long.

I want to witness the storm as the true Savannah emerges and unleashes her pent-up rage on the world.

Licking my lips, I taste the last remnants of her on my tongue.

I need more.

The door across the hall closes and I dart to the peephole to see who it is.

What the fuck?

Savannah's long hair and perfect ass come into view. She never leaves her apartment once she gets home.

Something is wrong.

Moving to the window, I watch as she walks

past her car, slowly striding down the sidewalk.

Did our kiss upset her enough to drive her from the apartment where it happened? If she thinks she's going to roam around the city in the dark, she's painfully mistaken.

The only good thing about living in this shitty apartment building is the ability to hear every time her door opens and closes.

I'm still dressed from earlier, so I put on my baseball cap and grab my keys and gun, locking the front door behind me as I leave. Jogging down the sidewalk, I finally spot her a few hundred feet ahead of me.

She spends the next twenty minutes lost in her head, as I follow closely behind. She's walking aimlessly and I curse as she makes a left at the corner market, heading down a shitty street known for drug activity.

The cops don't even patrol this road.

Fuck.

I could stop her, but it would only make things worse between us. If she feels cornered, she may run and of course I'll chase her.

She's not paying attention to her surroundings, so I'll keep her safe with my fists, my knife, or the pistol tucked in my waistband at my back. I never leave home without my forty-five.

You never know what kind of trouble you'll run into.

She's nearing the dead end when I hear it.

Catcalls.

My body tenses and my pace quickens, realizing I'll kill anyone who tries to hurt her.

A man approaches Savannah, his hands and arms spread as if to embrace her. She takes a step back, but he doesn't stop his pursuit.

Her expression is cold and disconnected.

I take off running towards her, but before I can get her attention, she rips her hand from her pocket.

In the blink of an eye, she sinks a knife into the side of his neck, blood spraying her face and chest.

Stopping in my tracks, I watch the man fall to the ground, clawing at his throat. She squats down beside him, pulling the knife from his neck, saying something too low for me to hear.

Fuck me.

Blood pools on the asphalt beneath him and she remains still, watching the life drain from his eyes. Her face is blank as she watches his chest rise and fall, until it deflates for the last time.

My mind is reeling, but everything stops when her green eyes meet mine, bright and full of satisfaction.

Her lively energy beats against me across the distance and my chest constricts when she smiles. My cock hardens painfully at the sight of her covered in blood and I know without a doubt, she's mine.

My timid little caterpillar has exploded from her cocoon and she's the brightest butterfly in the fucking sky.

She didn't need my protection. She's perfectly capable of taking care of herself but damn I'm glad I was here for the show.

We hold each other's gaze until she finally stands, sauntering towards me with a confidence I've never seen from her. I meet her halfway, gripping her by the throat, pulling her against me. My free hand flies to the back of her head, wrapping her ponytail around my fist. "You've done it now, little savage." Slamming our lips together, my tongue plunges inside her mouth, taking everything she has to give.

She arches her back, moaning as I deepen the kiss. I release her throat, sliding my hand down her back until I reach her ass. Gripping her tightly, I grind against her slowly, showing her exactly what she does to me.

A door creaks open in the distance, and I pull away from her abruptly. "We have to go." I grab her hand and we take off running, not slowing down until we're a few streets over.

It occurs to me once we're walking that she hasn't spoken a word since killing that guy. "Are you okay, baby?"

She meets my gaze, a serene look on her face. "I'm okay." She responds, her voice light and carefree.

Anyone else would be concerned with how she's reacting, but I've been in her shoes. I think my little savage just found her calm in the chaos.

"You followed me." It's not a question, but an

observation.

"I heard you leave. I couldn't let you roam the streets at night, alone." Pulling her closer, I wrap my arm around her shoulders.

She lets me do it, a small smile tugging at her lips. "I just killed a man."

"What happened?" I ask, unable to take my eyes off her.

"I'm sure you saw everything." She scoffs as the apartment building comes into view.

"Just because I saw you doesn't mean I heard what he said."

She rolls her eyes, making my cock twitch behind my jeans. I'm torn between reddening her delicious backside or sinking inside her from behind. Either way, my hands would be on her perfect ass.

"He said I'd be a popular little whore and earn him a lot of money. When I stepped back, he called me a skittish bitch and said he'd be happy to break me. I flicked my pocketknife open and let my instinct take over." She shrugs her shoulders as we make it to her front door, and she unlocks it.

My blood heats inside my veins and if the motherfucker wasn't already dead, I'd torture him slowly for talking to her like that. No one will ever disrespect her again. She's mine now and I always take care of what's mine.

Following her inside, she whirls around. "Did I say you could come in?" A faint smile tugs at her lips and I feel like I'm in an alternate universe.

Maybe playing death brought her to life.

I haven't had the pleasure of seeing Savannah's playful side and I'm ready for it. "I don't recall asking, little chaos."

Tilting her head to the side, she studies me. "Why do you call me that?"

Closing the door behind me, I flip the deadbolt, turning to face her again. "Your mind is chaos. I know you're fighting demons, Sav. Like seeks like."

She nods in understanding, and I know the day will likely come when she discovers my secrets.

The *reason* I'm here.

Even worse, *how* I got here.

She sits on the couch, and I take the seat next to her. Our knees touch but she doesn't pull away.

Damn, I should have coaxed her into murder months ago.

Reaching over, I pull the tie from her ponytail, satisfied when her long chocolate hair falls over her shoulders. "What did you say to him when you pulled out the knife?"

"No one else will break me."

Chapter Seven

Savannah

Something inside me snapped when that prick started spewing his nasty bullshit at me.

All my anger and dark thoughts boiled over until I exploded.

I plunged my pocketknife into his neck and the pop sound it made sent goosebumps erupting across my skin.

It was fucking euphoric.

In that moment, it felt like the devil himself possessed my body, satisfaction filling every cell as I watched the pathetic piece of shit choke on his own blood.

Am I finally having a psychotic break?

It's crossed my mind I should see a therapist, but I'm pretty sure if I go now, they'll have to report me to the police.

Oh well.

Of all the fantasies I've had in my brave moments, locked in my lonely apartment, I never thought I could actually take a life. I've dreamed about taking Colin's often, but I always figured I'd chicken out and he'd kill me first.

In killing someone who was a stain on society, I've found a sliver of hope in this life.

The feeling intensified as a moment of clarity took over and I scanned my surroundings. Imagine my surprise when I saw Declan, watching me with shock and awe on his face.

The adrenaline pumping through my veins settled as my feet carried me toward him. He met me halfway, devouring my mouth until I didn't remember where we were. A neighbor's door opening broke the spell, but I replayed the moment over and over on our way home.

I've kept everyone at bay, avoiding relationships at all costs. Nick was an exception, but it ended the same way.

In death.

Protecting myself from losing someone else I care about has been my goal for the past two years.

Declan has other plans though. He's trying to break down my walls and damn if it's not working. If I can kill to protect myself, I can kill to protect the ones I care about.

That thought alone gives me another bit of hope.

Running the comb through my wet hair, I take one last look in the mirror, freshly showered and free of blood splatter.

My skin has more color, and my eyes are brighter. Flipping the light off quickly, I open the door and head into my bedroom.

Declan is right when he says my mind is chaos, but part of me fears I've just opened pandora's box and I'm equally scared of what I will become.

My thoughts have gone from depressed and lonely to confident and hopeful in a matter of hours. It's scary to think how one event can change the way you think.

One *major* event.

His voice startles me as he sits on my bed. "Do you feel better?" His eyes roam down my body and my skin heats.

I'm wrapped in a towel, yet I feel completely naked under his heated gaze. My core tightens at his appraisal, watching his pearly white teeth graze his bottom lip. My thighs clench together, my heart threatening to beat out of my chest.

He stands from the bed, sauntering towards me like a wolf about to pounce on his prey. My feet move backwards, my back hitting the wall and I'm trapped. He doesn't stop until he's towering over me, and I tilt my head back to meet his gaze.

He places his hands on the wall on either side of my head, leaning into my body. "Answer me, little savage."

"W-what was the question?"

A wolfish grin lifts his lips and if I were wearing panties, they'd be soaked. Instead, it pools between my clenched thighs, stopping it from sliding down my trembling legs.

I've never reacted to anyone like this.

I'm twenty-one, but I'm also a virgin. There was never anyone I wanted to give my innocence to. Sure, I've kissed a guy or two, but that's as far as it went.

My traitorous body has my mind spiraling and all I can think about is Declan's hands all over me.

Fuck, I crave it.

His eyes darken, his voice dropping low. "Tell me you're okay."

"I'm okay. Well, probably not. I'll never be okay, but I feel better since I killed that guy. Oh my God! Did I just say that out loud. Fuck! I didn't mean-"

He spins his hat around with one hand, crushing his lips to mine. The warmth of his mouth cuts off my ramblings and I'm soon lost in the way his tongue moves against mine. My hands find his chest, fisting the fabric of his shirt, pulling him closer. He groans into my mouth, and I whimper as his hands slide down my sides, not stopping until he's gripping my ass. He pulls me close, grinding himself against me and I gasp.

I know nothing about dicks, but he feels *huge*. I wasn't great in anatomy class either, but I don't think that thing will fit inside me.

Jesus!

Why am I thinking about his dick inside of me?

While pushing the thought away for my own sanity, I just can't bring myself to push *him* away.

He massages my ass, kissing across my jaw, leaving a wet trail down my throat.

"Dex." I moan, sliding my fingers through his hair.

He stills, his eyes snapping to mine. He's looking for something, though I'm not sure what. He kisses me again; slower this time and it lures me into a place filled with lust and desire.

God, what is he doing to me?

He pulls away slowly and I whimper at the loss

of contact. As he moves away, my towel begins to unravel, but he grabs the corner, tucking it back in. "I need to go."

My stomach sinks.

Looking anywhere but at him, I wrap my arms around myself. "Oh, okay."

He lifts my chin with his finger. "Hey."

My eyes dart around the room. I'll die of humiliation if I have to see his rejection.

"Look at me." He demands and after a few moments I do.

His face softens. "I'm leaving because if I don't, this will go too far. You've been through some shit tonight and you need time to process. Believe me, little chaos. Once I start with you, I won't stop."

My body relaxes. "Okay."

He pulls me into his chest, cradling the back of my head. He leans down, whispering against my ear. "I'm always here." Gripping my chin, he turns my head, kissing me senseless again.

If I thought my mind was chaotic before, this man takes it up a notch.

He's consuming me and while I've been fighting it desperately, I can't tonight.

I'll let him suffocate me with his kiss.

I'll let him burn me alive with his touch.

He pulls away slowly, picking up my phone from the nightstand. His fingers move quickly, a ding sounding in his pocket. "You have my number now. Call or text if you need anything."

He leaves my bedroom and I follow behind

him closely. Opening the door, he turns to say something, but grins instead. "Goodnight, little savage."

"Goodnight, Dex."

The door clicks as he closes it and I lock it before returning to my bedroom. Slipping on a t-shirt and panties, I slide into bed, thinking about the last few hours.

Surprisingly, I'm not worried about getting caught. Dex told me it was a known drug neighborhood, so the cops will just assume it was a drug deal gone wrong.

My phone dings beside me and I pick it up, squinting at the bright screen. A message pops up and I immediately grin to myself.

King: Are you in bed, little one?

No one's ever called me anything except my name. My dad would call me 'kiddo', and my mom would call me 'sweetheart', but that's it. Dex's endearments make me feel tingly like a teenage girl and I can't help but roll my eyes at myself.

Me: Who is this?

King: That will earn you a spanking, little chaos.

The thought of him reddening my ass makes my cheeks heat and I burrow myself deeper under the covers.

Me: That doesn't sound so bad.

King: Do you normally agree to spankings from strangers, baby?

Me: Depends on how dirty they talk to me.

Who the fuck am I and what happened to the terrified woman I woke up as this morning? There's no way I changed this drastically in the last few hours.

Definitely a psychotic break.

King: How you tempt me, naughty girl.

Me: Why?

King: Look at my name in your phone. You're my queen.

My heart stops and I swallow slowly. This guy is nuts. He doesn't even know me. If he did, he'd run in the other direction. But I can't stop the smile that tugs at my lips.

Me: You don't know me, Declan.

King: I know you better than you think. But we can play twenty questions if it will make you feel better.

Me: Okay. How old are you?

King: Twenty-eight.

Me: I'm twenty-one.

King: I know.

Me: Where are you from?

King: Bridgetown, you?

Me: Taylor's Cove.

Shit. I shouldn't have told him that.

King: I've been there. Nice little town.

Me: Yeah. It used to be. What's your last name?

King: Archer. Yours?

Me: Callahan.

Guilt claws at my insides, lying to him makes me feel sick. We don't know each other, so I'm not sure why it bothers me so much.

King: Get some sleep Sav Callahan from Taylor's Cove.

Me: You too, Declan Archer from Bridgetown.

Tossing my phone onto the nightstand, my usual worst case scenario thoughts come to mind.

What if I fall for Dex?

How do I hide my past from him?

What if Colin finds me?

Now that I've killed someone, will I be able to kill him?

After tossing and turning for hours, I finally drift to sleep imagining Dex's lips on my skin again.

Chapter Eight

Declan

I'm still awake when Savannah leaves to go to work.

How the hell could I sleep after tasting her sweet lips against mine?

Her door slams and I stop myself from going outside. Instead, I groan while pushing myself off the couch. I watch her leave from the window, my stomach sinking as she pulls out of the parking lot.

Shit.

I'm like a sad puppy, pathetically waiting for its owner to return home.

My phone rings and I pull it from my pocket, dragging my sorry ass away from the window. "Yeah?"

"Somebody's chipper this morning." Jase says sarcastically and I immediately regret answering the call.

"It's too early for your bullshit, Hamilton. What do you want?"

There's a shuffling sound before the line goes silent. "Hello?"

"Hey Dex, excuse my husband. He's mad because I called dibs on shooting our new mark." Rage explains and I smile, imagining the death glare she's giving him right now.

"No worries, killer. Who are you murdering today?" I chuckle, my mood lighter now that Jase is catching hell from his fiery wife.

I'll never forget the day I met Rage. She stood in a room full of hitmen, confidence radiating off her and a no bullshit attitude. Jase was worried we wouldn't accept her into our organization, but he was mistaken. We were all drawn to her like a moth to a flame. While Jase and I are the youngest in our group, the older guys were smitten after she spoke only a few words. "I don't particularly like people, but I want to kill bad guys with you."

The rest is history.

She's as capable as any of us when it comes to killing marks, maybe even more so. She loves the job and we're like a little family of killers, Rage being our mama bear. She keeps us in line, especially her husband. She checks in on us and offers to help with every job that comes across the desk.

"God, Dex. The guy is such a piece of shit. He sold his own daughter to the mob to pay off a gambling debt. Now he's started kidnapping girls to give them every time he owes them money."

The fire in her voice makes me smile. I know she will save every girl she can. If she can't, then she'll kill every motherfucker connected to their disappearances or their death. "Make it hurt, little hitwoman."

Hearing Jase groan in the background makes me chuckle and I realize I'm on speaker phone. "Why did you call me this early, bossman?"

"Our little hitwoman is nosey." He retorts and I

hear the smile in his voice.

Asshole.

"Shut up, Jase. I hear you have a crush on our little damsel in distress, Dex." She laughs, but something claws at my chest.

The need to defend her.

"She's not a damsel in distress. She stabbed a guy in the fucking throat yesterday for talking shit." I grit out, my temper flaring.

"What the fuck?" Jase shouts and I regret telling him instantly.

"No one saw us. I got her out of there right after it happened."

"Us? Why the hell were you there?" I hear his teeth grinding through the phone and it amps up my possessive side.

"Because she was upset and wandered off by herself. There's no way in hell I was leaving her alone." I growl.

The line falls silent, and I check my screen to make sure the call is still connected.

Jase clears his throat, and I can only imagine the silent conversation they're having. "Be careful, Dex. Call me if you need anything. Understand?"

Sighing heavily, I scrub my hand down my face. He's my boss, but more than that, he's my friend. He's helped shape me into the man I am today. The months he was gone while Malcolm ran the show were hell. We weren't close then, but after he returned with Rage, we developed a friendship, a brotherhood. "Thanks, Hamilton."

Ending the call, I flop down on the couch, my mind racing.

Savannah has me so fucked up, I'm willing to go head-to-head with my brother.

My head falls to the back of the couch as images of her play on repeat in my mind.

Her gorgeous body.

Those beautiful, haunted eyes.

The sweet taste of her lips.

The softness of her skin.

My body finally relaxes, and I doze off, imagining her curled up beside me.

Chapter Nine

Savannah

I'm on my way home after a long ass day at work.

My mind drifts to thoughts of self-reflection, which normally makes me nauseous.

While despair, guilt and possibly ending my life usually fill my head, something has changed.

Experiencing a fraction of hope when I stabbed that bastard in the throat yesterday, emotions I've long buried slowly make their way back to the surface.

I'm bitter.

My family was taken from me.

I'm scorned.

My own flesh and blood took them from me.

I'm fucking angry.

An image of Dylan pops in my head and my knuckles turn white from my grip on the steering wheel.

I want vengeance.

I want to rip Colin's beating heart from his chest.

I want to be the last thing he sees as he takes his last breath.

Eye for an eye, motherfucker.

Almost missing the turn for my apartment building, I realize I'm panting, on the verge of what some might think is a panic attack.

Far from it.

This is what fucking fury feels like and I embrace this shit with every cell in my body.

I'm no longer this depressed shell of a girl who can't function because she's overcome with grief.

Killing that guy awakened something inside me.

Something long overdue.

It's raw, primal and clawing to break free. My cage has been rattled and I'm ready to fight.

For myself.

For my family.

For my life.

As I pull into my usual parking spot, there's two guys standing at the edge of the walkway. Turning the car off, I lean over to grab my purse.

Reaching under the seat, I pull out the tire thumper. I bought it for protection in case Colin ever found me while I was away from home.

My fingers wrap around the cool wood handle, and I slide it into my lap. It looks like a miniature baseball bat, and I thought it was a good choice for a weapon. Besides, I didn't think the cops would think twice about it if I was ever pulled over.

Glancing at Declan's window, it's dark inside. He must not be home.

Odd.

I think I've seen him every day since he moved in.

Gripping the handle, I push open the door, tightening my hold on the tire thumper behind my back. As my feet touch the asphalt, I hear one of the men say, *"That's her."*

My stomach tightens as I pretend to ignore them, hyper aware of my surroundings. They're average build, average height and oh so forgettable. My newfound courage rises as I reach the front of my car, stepping onto the sidewalk.

"Whoa, bitch." The one on the left snarls and I come to a stop.

Have I gone crazy?

The switch has finally flipped, and I've lost my mind.

Better this than what you were.

My eyes land on the one who called me a bitch, and he blinks in surprise at my wide smile.

The one on the right looks me over, a sinister smile on his face. "She's the one I saw running after Johnny got stabbed. I didn't get a good look at the guy, but I saw her."

My blood runs cold at the thought of someone spotting Declan with me.

"Kill them!" A little voice whispers in my mind and for once I agree.

"He's right. I'm the one who stabbed ol' Johnny boy in the throat. What are you going to do about it?" I snap and they both freeze, blinking rapidly.

Wasn't expecting that, huh boys?

The one on the left snarls like a rabid dog, lunging straight for me. I sidestep him quickly, swinging the tire thumper through the air, hitting him across the back. He falls to the ground howling, and I bust him in the back of the skull. He's out cold, possibly dead.

I'm okay with the latter.

Turning to face the other guy, I taunt him. "Come on, fuck boy. Let's see what you got."

He makes a pathetic growling sound before running towards me. "You fucking bitch! You'll be begging for death when I'm done with you."

He's in mid sprint and I move out of the way but lose all grace when I trip over his friend's outstretched arm. I hit the ground, landing on my ass and pain shoots up my spine, making my mouth water and my eyes blur. The impact forces the thumper from my hand, and I watch as it rolls away, not stopping until it's under my car, out of reach.

Well shit.

The guy's pace doesn't slow and when he moves to jump on top of me, his entire body is jerked back, and he squeals like a little pig.

Blinking a few times to refocus, Declan is holding the bastard in the air, pinning him against the side of the building. He doesn't have a shirt on, and I shamelessly take in every corded muscle from the top of his shoulders down to his torso. He's covered in tattoos and my fingers twitch against the asphalt, begging to touch him.

Fuck, he's a magnificent sight.

"My apartment. Now." The command in his voice has me slowly rising to my feet, wincing at the sharp tingles of pain shooting down my back.

Risking another glance at him, I stand frozen, debating whether I should be terrified or elated at the expression on his face.

Murder.

His jaw is clenched, his body taut and his eyes are so black he looks possessed by a demon. His arm bulges as he holds the guy in place, his feet dangling above the ground.

"Now!" He barks and I hurry to his apartment, shutting and locking the door behind me. Heading for the couch, I quickly sit down, closing my eyes, focusing on the rhythm of my heart.

What a rush.

I would've been screwed if Declan didn't save my ass, but I was having fun before I tripped over the other asshole's arm.

I wonder if he's dead...

Once my body has relaxed a bit, I turn my head and glance around his apartment.

Damn near empty.

Is this how single guys live?

My apartment is sparse in décor because I have a shitty job and I'm broke.

Maybe Declan is too. I've never asked what he does for a living.

Standing from the couch, I give myself a tour. The living room has a couch, coffee table and television. Heading into the kitchen, there's nothing but a stove and refrigerator. There's nothing on the walls. I mean, no photos, no art, nothing.

Moving to the window that faces the parking lot, I don't see Declan or the other two guys. Worry fills my stomach with knots, but I know if I leave this apartment to go check, he'll lose his shit.

Making my way down the hall, I peek into the bathroom, and it looks normal. It smells of his spicy cologne, making me grin as I breathe deeply. Moving along, his bedroom door is open, and I walk inside the room. It's another plain room, only a bed with a nightstand on each side. There's no dresser or anything.

As I turn around to look in his closet, I gasp, the blood in my veins turning to ice.

On his closet door is a large brown bulletin board, filled with pictures.

Of me.

What the fuck?

My mind spins at a dizzying speed and I think I'm going to be sick. I stare at the photos on the board, a reflection of myself over the past few months.

Sadness.

Defeat.

Depression.

Everything I despise about myself is captured in these snapshots.

My stomach churns and I try to still my nerves to keep from vomiting.

Declan has been stalking me.

He's lied to me and once again, I realize I can't trust my own instincts.

The worst thought possible fills my mind.

Is he working for Colin? Was he sent to kill me?

The will to live surges through me like never before and as the front door opens and closes in the distance, I find my resolve.

If anyone tries to kill me, *they* will die first.

That includes Declan Archer.

Chapter Ten

Declan

I had my alarm set to wake me up when Savannah usually gets home.

Getting up from the couch, I fumble around in the darkness, heading to the bathroom.

Once I'm finished, I go back to the living room, looking out of the window to see if she's home yet.

Blinking rapidly, my eyes struggle to focus on what I'm seeing.

Two men.

One on the ground, Savannah swinging a mini bat down on his skull.

She turns toward the second man and as he approaches her, she trips over the guy on the ground.

I'm moving before anything else happens. Swinging the door open, I rush down the steps and as he lunges for her, I grab him mid-air, swinging him into the building.

The breath whooshes out of him, and I grip him by the throat, pushing him up the brick wall, adrenaline and rage fueling my strength.

Savannah listened to me, running to my apartment, but I could tell she was in pain where she hit the ground.

After she closes the door, I drag the guy around the back of the building. He's begging and pleading for his life, but I tune it out.

He wanted to hurt my girl.

He's going to die.

I don't have a weapon on me, so I do the next best thing.

A loud crack ripples through the air as I snap the motherfucker's neck.

He falls to the ground, and I drag him behind the bushes against the building to hide him for the time being.

Jogging around front, I check the other guy's pulse.

He's dead.

Good girl.

Lifting him over my shoulder, I carry him around back, dumping his body on top of his friend.

Pulling out my phone, I send Jase a text, telling him I need a cleanup quickly. I give him a quick rundown of what happened and head back to my apartment to check on Savannah. Pulling my keys from my pocket, I open the front door, closing it behind me.

There's no sign of her so I move towards the back of the unit.

"They're dead, little savage." As I walk through my bedroom door, she stands in the middle of the room with her back to me.

Staring at photos of herself.

Fuck!

I didn't think about the board when I told her to come to my apartment. I had plans to take it down so she could come over, but it slipped my mind.

"Savannah-" Her full name slips out and she whirls around, hurt and betrayal in her eyes.

"Who the fuck are you?" She seethes and, in this moment, I see the *real* Savannah Banks.

There's a flame simmering in her eyes, peeking through the excess of emotions she's experienced over the past few days. Her spirit may be shattered but there's an inferno beneath her pain that is unscathed.

I saw her come back to life when she killed that asshole downtown.

There was fear in her eyes earlier, but I saw beyond it, glimpsing the adrenaline and thrill that made her fight.

When the day comes, I'll be here to witness the moment she unleashes all the chaos inside her.

It'll be a gorgeous sight when she sets herself free, condemning us all to her hell.

I'll embrace every moment of it and beg for more.

The way she's staring me down, I may not have to wait long.

"Is Declan even your name, fucker?" She grits out, pushing past me, leaving the bedroom.

I don't know where to start, but she can't leave this apartment without knowing I'm on her side. "Savannah, stop! Calm down and I'll explain everything." I bark and find out immediately it was the wrong thing to say.

Never tell a woman to calm down.

She stops abruptly by the pantry, reaching for the broom. Spinning around, she stalks towards me, her rage pulsing around us like strong zaps of electricity.

Fuck, she's beautiful.

While I'm completely screwed, I'm also the hardest I've ever been in my life. My cock strains against my jeans and I'd give anything to taste every inch of her fury, even if it's directed at me.

My hands clench, desperate to touch the dark goddess in front of me.

Those thoughts are short lived though as she swings the broom through the air, the handle connecting with my bicep, pain shooting down my arm.

"Explain what? That you're a fucking creeper and you've been stalking me?" She hits me with the broom again, striking my thigh this time.

She swings again, aiming for my head, but I rip it from her grip before she makes contact.

Her chest heaves, her perky tits bouncing with every breath. "Did he send you? Are you waiting for the opportunity to kill me?"

All thoughts disappear as I stand frozen under her scrutiny. "You think I could hurt you?"

She blinks twice, her empty hands fisting at her sides. "You fucking lied to me!"

She whirls towards the door, but I grip her waist, pushing her against it with my body. "I didn't fucking lie. I omitted the truth. I'll give you a short time to be pissed off and have your tantrum. You won't listen to anything I say right now anyway."

Pressing into her harder, she pushes back against me, trying to break away. "Fuck you!"

Chuckling darkly, I whisper against her ear. "Listen to me carefully because I will not repeat myself. I don't work for your motherfucking uncle. I will never hurt you. I'm here to protect you. The quicker you get that through your head, the better off we'll both be."

It takes everything I have to let her go. She slowly turns around, the fury in her eyes fading a bit. She closes the gap between us and just when I think she's beginning to understand, she swings. Her tiny fist connects with my jaw, and I'm impressed with how much force she packs within her small frame.

"Leave me alone. I don't need your protection." She grits out.

Before I can blink again, she storms out of the door, and I'm left standing here with a throbbing jaw and the shame of having my ass whooped with a broom.

"Do you need to borrow my pink lawn chair so you can sit outside her door and demand her attention? It won Rage over." Jase asks and I want to choke him through the phone.

"No, I don't want your fucking lawn chair, asshole." I grumble.

I couldn't sleep last night because of what happened. Savannah is mine and the fact she's upset is killing me.

I get it.

This whole thing was a shock and a complete invasion of her privacy. But she needs to understand we were trying to protect her.

In the process, I've fallen for her.

She's mine whether she likes it or not. She has to forgive me. I've accepted all her lies because I know it made her feel safe. I need her to accept mine and understand it was for her own good.

This is so fucked up.

"Dex, go apologize and tell her the truth. You said it yourself, she's strong and smart. She'll understand." Jase reasons and I groan because I know he's right.

"Any suggestions on how I should grovel?" I ask, already regretting the question.

"With lots of orgasms." He chuckles and I pinch the bridge of my nose, wondering why in the hell I called him.

"Yeah, thanks." I say, ending the call.

Sitting on the couch, I play through different scenarios that would make Savannah understand and forgive me.

I don't think flowers will work.

Cooking her dinner probably won't either.

Finally settling on a plan, I head to my bedroom, grabbing my duffle bag from the closet. Tossing it on the bed, I close the door, staring at the board with her pictures on it.

Slowly, I remove each photo, placing them in a neat pile inside my nightstand drawer. Removing the bulletin board, I toss it in the back of the closet.

Unzipping the duffle bag, I search until I find my lock picking kit.

Breaking and entering it is…

Chapter Eleven

Savannah

I'm fucking miserable.

No matter how I try to push him out of my mind, all I can think about is Declan.

I'm so angry with him, but after getting a few hours' sleep, I'm thinking more clearly now.

Understanding why he didn't tell me the truth does little to soothe the sting.

I miss him.

And I'm fucking exhausted.

My mental health is up in the air at this point.

All this emotional shit has taken its toll and I'm just so tired.

I'm glad to be off work today and tomorrow.

I'm not innocent in this. I know that.

Where he withheld the truth from me, I've flat out lied to him. He accepted my lies while he knew the truth the entire time and he still wanted to be with me.

Maybe I should forgive him and move past this?

It's something to think about anyway.

After a nap…

Startling awake, I shoot up in bed, my hand flying to my chest.

My eyes dart from one side of the room to the other, the soft light from the lamp alerting me of the man sitting across from me in the chair.

"You were having a nightmare. I wanted to wake you, but I didn't want to get stabbed." It sounds like a joke, but the grave look on Declan's face says otherwise.

"How did you get in here?" I croak, my throat dry from sleep.

"I picked your locks." He shrugs.

I should've known. "I wish you would've woken me up." I murmur, leaning against the headboard.

"Maybe I want to know what torments you." He responds, his voice colder than usual.

"You mean you don't already? You're a pretty shitty stalker then." Rolling my eyes, he stands up, pulling the chair closer to the bed.

He sits once again, propping his elbows on his knees, lacing his fingers together. "I'm going to tell you a story and you're going to listen. When I'm finished, if you want me to leave, I will."

I'm torn.

My mind screams to throw him out and never speak to him again. He lied to me, and I can't handle anymore bullshit in my life.

But my stupid fucking heart has feelings for this asshole, and I truly believe he doesn't work for Colin. My heart be damned, I don't believe he'd hurt me. I lied to him too and at the end of the day, we both lied for my protection.

What a fucked-up situation.

I follow my gut instinct. I've always ignored

it in the past, not trusting my own intuition, but with Declan, I'll listen and pray it doesn't backfire. "I'm all ears."

He leans back in the chair, his demeanor relaxed other than the cold expression on his face. He's silent for a few minutes and I wonder what he's thinking.

"I was a troubled kid. The details are for another day, but I had it rough growing up. One day when I was sixteen, I pickpocketed a guy and before I could run, two of his men grabbed me. I was sure he'd kill me once I saw his face. Charles Lutz was the boss of this city. Nothing happened here without him knowing. Most people loved him for how much he helped the community, but they didn't know the *real* Charles."

He gazes at the ceiling, a faint smile on his lips like he's lost in a memory. I shift down the bed, propping my head on my palm, watching his expression as this happy thought fills his mind. The rustling of the blankets catches his attention, and he continues.

"Obviously he didn't kill me. But he did kill people. Bad people. He had a team of men he trusted, and they formed an organization that took out the crooked politicians, sex traffickers, and anyone else that posed a threat to our peaceful city. He offered me a chance to be something more than a petty thief running from my home life. He took me in and gave me something to focus on, something to excel at. He had me train with his best man, Jase. He taught me how to shoot and how to become invisible. At eighteen, they told me I was ready, and I never looked back."

"So, you're a hitman?" I ask.

His eyes bore into mine. "Yes."

I'm silent for a moment before I sit up in the bed, facing him. "I can see you killing the bad guys. From the moment I first spoke to you, you gave off protector vibes."

He blinks a couple of times. "You're not scared?"

Snorting out a laugh, I shake my head. "No, I'm not scared of you, Declan. I'm confused as to what this has to do with me though."

He watches me closely and I shift on the mattress. Did he want me to be scared or is he stunned that I'm not?

"Colin Banks ended up on our radar after he killed your family."

Hearing the words from someone else's mouth is a shock to my system.

He notices, leaning forward. "I'm sorry, Savannah."

Clearing my throat, I pull myself together. "It's fine. Keep going."

He eyes me cautiously before leaning back in the chair again. "He wanted your father's gunrunning business. He knew the contracts with the MC's and mid-level drug organizations were a small gold mine, but Colin was greedy. After taking over the operation, he started trafficking women. We managed to turn some of his guys for information and while interrogating them, we learned of his obsession."

"His obsession with what?" I whisper, already knowing the answer.

"You."

Blowing out a breath, I flip onto my back, staring at the same spot on the ceiling he was a few moments ago. While I'm glad he's telling me the truth, I can't help the ache in my chest.

"So, this was a job." I say flatly, trying to hide the hurt from my voice.

"It started as a job. My mission was to hunt down your uncle and take him out. Everything changed the moment I saw you, Savannah. I knew I'd do anything to protect you. Anything to make you mine."

Finding his gaze, I see the truth in his eyes, and it removes any doubt I have about us.

Now, I just have to worry about Colin and his sick fucking obsession with murdering me. I want the bastard dead.

I've stayed hidden for two years.

If I swallow my fear and start looking for him now, he'll find me. He's well connected, and I'll be like a beacon in the night.

"I don't know what to do." I whisper into the quiet room.

Declan leans forward, lacing his fingers with mine. "He broke your trust. He shattered your world. He killed your family. For all those things, he *will* die. Once I've put him in the ground, it'll all be over. I hope you'll let me in. Let me give you the happiness you deserve."

Tears threaten to fall as a calmness I've never experienced settles in my chest.

I'm not alone.

Not anymore.

Reaching for the empty side of my bed, I pull back the blanket, quirking my brow. He wastes no time removing his shoes before climbing in beside me. Laying on his side, he wraps his arm around my waist, pulling me against him.

Sighing with contentment, I listen to the sound of his heartbeat.

We're quiet for a while until he speaks again, his lips moving against the top of my head. "You've been sad for so long, baby. Let me help you unleash the beautiful chaos in your mind. I've seen a glimpse of who you really are. The hidden darkness in your heart. It's okay to be angry, Savannah. But you can't let it eat you alive. Let it out. Guide it." He kisses my temple as I look up at him. "Give me your pain. I'll carry it for you."

Tears burn my eyes, and my mind loses all functionality.

This is too much.

He is too much.

But damn if he's not everything I've ever wanted.

Gripping the back of his neck, I pull him down, devouring his mouth. There are no words for what

I'm feeling right now. It's a frenzy of emotions and there's only one thing I'm certain of.

I need him.

He grunts in surprise, quickly recovering as he takes control of the kiss, my back pressing into the mattress as he rolls on top of me.

Wrapping my legs around his waist, he growls into my mouth. "Fuck, Savannah. I thought I lost you."

He grinds himself against my core and I moan into the kiss, desperate to give him the one thing no one has taken from me.

My virginity.

His large hands travel down my sides, gripping the hem of my shirt. He lifts it slowly and I raise my upper body as he pulls it over my head. His mouth is back on mine before the shirt has time to hit the floor. His fingers skim the sides of my breasts, moving down my torso until he reaches my panties.

He groans into my mouth as he grips the fabric tightly, ripping it from my body.

I gasp at the sting, and he grins against my lips. "There's no way I was going to move your legs from where they are."

Huffing a laugh, I sober quickly realizing I'm naked in front of a man for the first time in my life. Pushing at his chest, he stops immediately, his gaze finding mine.

"I've never done this before." I whisper, heat flooding my face.

He grins. "I had a feeling, baby. I'm going to take care of you."

He kisses me slowly, licking inside my mouth with lazy strokes. I match his pace, losing myself in his touch. He moves his lips across my jaw, down my throat, my body trembling beneath him. He moves lower, licking a trail between my breasts.

My back arches as he sucks my nipple into his warm mouth, his teeth grazing the tight point. He moves to my other breast, repeating the action and a deep moan leaves my chest. Pleasure tears through my body, lighting up every nerve ending. My pussy clenches, desperate to be filled. All the new sensations are the sweetest torture, and I want more.

"Dex, please." I whimper, needing something, anything to soothe the burn inside me.

"Shhh. I've got you." He whispers, his hot tongue trailing down my stomach, his short beard scraping across my skin until he reaches my pussy.

He grips my thighs, spreading them wide, making room for his broad shoulders. He finds my gaze as he slides one finger down my slit and I moan, my hips jerking, begging for more.

His fingers spread me open, my skin on fire, completely exposed to him. "So pink and swollen. You're needy for me, aren't you, little chaos?"

"Yes!" I hiss, wiggling my hips, searching for more friction.

He chuckles darkly, leaning forward, swiping his tongue through my wetness and I snap.

My fingers dive into his hair, gripping it tightly, pulling him closer. He spears me with his tongue, and I grind against his face, needy whimpers escaping my lips.

His tongue is the fucking devil and I'm aching to fall into the pits of hell.

I've never felt anything this good in my life.

"That's it, baby. Ride my fucking face." He demands and I obey the demon between my legs.

His thumb circles my clit, and my vision darkens at the corners. My lower belly coils tighter as he sinks two fingers inside me, his tongue replacing his thumb, sucking my clit hard.

The world stops as my vision dims, and I scream his name until my throat feels raw. My thighs clench around his head and for a moment I'm scared I'll suffocate him, but his fingers still pump inside me, drawing out my orgasm.

Why have I never done this before?

Only he can make you feel like this.

My body relaxes and I release him, but he doesn't move, his tongue dipping in and out of my pussy, drinking every drop of my release. My hips rock against his face, unable to stop chasing this feeling.

He rises to his knees, and my mouth goes dry as he removes his shirt.

Fuck me.

I have a better view now than I did the other night. He has more ridges than I can count and more ink on his skin than my tongue can possibly trace in one night.

He catches me with my mouth hanging open and he grins. "Do you like what you see, baby?"

Words fail me so I just nod my head. Lifting myself from the mattress, I reach for his belt. My hands are trembling so badly, my fingers won't cooperate, and I huff in frustration.

He catches my hands, moving them out of the way. I watch in fascination as he unbuckles his belt, removing the leather from his jeans with a quick flick of his wrist.

I think I just got pregnant.

His sinful grin widens as he stands from the bed, unbuttoning his pants, sliding them down his legs along with his boxers. After kicking them off with his feet, my eyes focus on his enormous cock and the large hand stroking it slowly. The light catches something shiny and I gasp when I realize what it is.

He has multiple piercings on the underside of his dick.

Jesus.

I'm second guessing myself. Giving my virginity to a man with a huge cock and piercings may not be the best idea. I'm pretty sure you're supposed to work your way up to something like this.

As our gazes collide, his eyes beg me to trust him.

After all the bullshit over the past few days, we both lied to each other with one common goal.

My safety.

That alone gives me the courage to accept him and to trust him.

"Um, what is all that?" I ask, pointing at his dick.

He chuckles. "It's called a Jacob's Ladder."

"Why did you do it? Were you a playboy?" The jealous words fall from my lips before I can stop them.

He grins. "I was never a playboy. Never wanted to be. I got them for the pain, and I was bored."

Okay then.

Lowering my back to the mattress, I open my legs, the throbbing between them almost painful. My body knows where he belongs and she's opening up like a flower to let him inside.

"Your body knows you're mine." He growls, watching my pussy as he climbs on the bed, coming to hover above me.

"Maybe she knows you're mine." I sass, my breath coming in short pants as the head of his cock bumps my sensitive clit.

"There's no doubt about that, little chaos. I fucking belong to you." He groans, sliding his cock through my wetness.

My chest and pussy both constrict at his words, and I wrap my hand around the back of his neck, pulling him down for a kiss. He pushes his tongue past my lips, stealing my breath with urgent strokes.

He breaks the kiss after a few moments,

breathing heavily. Pressing his forehead to mine, he gives me a pained look. "This is going to hurt, baby."

"I know." I've heard how sex always hurts the first time, but once you adjust it will feel good.

Hopefully.

"Tell me to stop if it's too much." He groans, the head of his cock pushing past my entrance.

As he stretches me, the burning sensation is almost too much. My eyes scrunch closed as he pushes forward until he reaches the resistance of my barrier. "Look at me. I want to see you as I take what's mine."

My eyes snap open and he grunts as my pussy contracts. Leaning down, he kisses the hell out of me and just as my body relaxes, his hips punch forward, claiming my innocence.

"Fuck!" I scream, tears leaking from the corners of my eyes. My back arches off the mattress, my body rejecting the intrusion.

He's going to rip me apart.

"Are you okay?" He asks, not moving, giving me time to adjust. Lowering his head, he licks and sucks my throat, pinching my nipples, trying to distract me. After a few moments, the pain subsides, replaced with something deep and carnal.

Rolling my hips, there's a dull ache deep within, but the need for him to fuck me overshadows everything else. "Dex, please." I moan, rolling my hips again.

He growls against my throat, the vibration going straight to my pussy. Pulling back until just the tip remains, he plunges inside me harder, deeper.

Sliding one arm underneath me, he pins me against him, while his other hand grips my throat. He doesn't apply too much pressure, just enough to show he's in control. Wrapping my legs around his waist, I scrape my nails down his back as he ruts inside me like a wild animal. His piercings drag along my inner walls, and I clench at the sensation.

A pussy massage.

"Fuck, Savannah. Your tight pussy is better than I ever imagined." He murmurs, his deep voice making my body tremble.

Another orgasm is building quickly, and I know it will shatter me from the inside out. "I'm going to come again."

"Come on my cock, little savage. Give me what's mine."

His filthy mouth pushes me over the edge, and I sob his name as my body convulses and everything darkens around me. My body arches against him as he roars his own release, no doubt the neighbors hearing him. Pride swells in my chest knowing I did that to this dangerous man.

An assassin.

My protector.

He falls on top of me, his heavy weight like a security blanket. He shifts his weight to his forearms, gazing deeply into my eyes. The intensity in his stare stills my breathing and we're suspended in a moment of time where only we exist.

"You fucking own me, Savannah. I'll never let you go." He declares, fear and hope mingling together in my mind.

"What if I run?" I blurt out without thinking.

"I'll chase you, little chaos. I'll always find you." He grins wickedly.

His cock twitches inside me and I moan wanting more, but as he slides out of me, the lingering pain settles in.

He gets off the bed, picks me up, and carries me to the bathroom. Wrapping my legs around his waist and my arms around his neck, he turns the faucet on to the bathtub. His other hand grips my ass, holding me tightly as the tub fills with water.

"A warm bath will help with the pain." He soothes, running his hands down my back.

I give him a sleepy grin as I slide down his body, settling on my feet. "Get in with me?"

He looks at the tub and then at me. "It's going to be a tight fit, but we'll make it work."

Turning off the faucet, he grips my hand, helping me step in. Once I'm settled, I scoot forward as he climbs in behind me.

He was right, it's a tight fit, but I like it. He pulls me into his chest, pressing his lips against my temple. My head falls back as I soak in his warmth.

I could get used to this...

Chapter Twelve

Savannah

He grabs the body wash, squirting some on the washcloth and gently lathers my body. The past few hours have damn near given me whiplash.

Maybe I shouldn't have forgiven Dex so easily, but I'm drawn to him. There's no rhyme or reason for the feelings I'm developing for him, but it feels right. Giving myself to him tonight only intensified everything and I wonder if it did the same for him.

How can my life go from utter shit to this so quickly?

"You're thinking pretty loud, baby."

Turning my head slightly, he's watching me closely. "The past few hours have been a lot."

The worry in his eyes grows. "Is that a bad thing?"

"No, it's not a bad thing. I'm just processing." Moving my hand from the side of the tub, I reach up, cupping his cheek.

He covers my hand with his own, squeezing it reassuringly. "How about you talk to me, and I'll help you work it out?" His hand dips between my legs, the cloth sending tingles along my skin as it caresses my oversensitive pussy.

"Um, I'll try. I haven't had anyone to talk to in a while, so I'm not used to this." My breath turns choppy, and he smirks, knowing what he's doing to me.

He removes his hand, his lips close to my ear. "I want to know everything, Savannah, but I'll take whatever you can give me."

Slowly and quite awkwardly, I turn in the tub, facing him. He scoots forward a little, gripping my legs, and wraps them around his waist.

His hard cock bobs in the water between us, but he ignores it.

We gaze at each other for a few minutes and my chest constricts, knowing this man is in my life for a reason.

Whether he saves me from myself or condemns me to heartbreak remains to be seen.

Droplets of water cascade down his muscular chest and the need to touch him everywhere is overwhelming. "Can I wash you?"

His eyes widen in surprise, but he grins. "You can do whatever you want to me, little chaos. You never have to ask."

Squeezing more body wash onto the cloth, I begin rubbing circles across his skin. Maybe having something to focus on will make what I'm about to say easier. "My dad was a good man. I know he did illegal shit, but he wasn't a bad guy. He loved us all so much and he made sure we knew it."

Moving the cloth lower, I'm momentarily distracted, but he smirks, taking it from me. "I'll finish this. You keep talking."

I don't know what to do with my hands as I watch him intently. He washes quickly, before gripping my wrists, pressing them to his chest. "Go on, little one."

Exhaling heavily, my mind is back in the past. Where it's usually unbearable, the feel of Dex's skin beneath my palms centers me. "My mom was a bad bitch. She loved us fiercely, but she also didn't let us get too wild." I snort and a small smile plays on Dex's lips as he rubs soothing circles on my wrists.

"I fought *a lot* in school. I didn't take shit off people, but most of my fights were from protecting other kids. My mom got fed up after a while and told my dad to deal with me. I just knew my ass was in trouble, but he surprised me. Every night before dinner, he took me down to the basement and taught me how to fight. Mom was pissed, but I caught her in the doorway a few times watching me, smiling. I don't think she wanted her little girl fighting, but at the same time, she was proud I could protect myself."

Dex chuckles and it makes me smile. "Mom's usually want their princesses in tiaras, not breaking noses."

"True." I grin and notice the water is getting cold. "Should we get out now?"

He smacks me on the ass. "Up you go. Dry off and get in bed. We're not finished talking."

Rolling my eyes, I stand and step out of the tub before a harder slap lands across my ass cheek. "What the fuck, Declan?" The sting sets in, and I know there's a handprint on my ass.

He stands up in all his naked glory, stepping from the tub. Glaring daggers, I throw a towel at him.

He catches it, stepping into me, gripping my jaw. "Don't roll your eyes at me, little one."

Gritting my teeth, I grip his cock in my hand, squeezing slightly, the piercings pushing between my fingers. "Don't be so fucking bossy."

He groans, pushing me against the wall, devouring my mouth until I lose my breath. My irritation dissipates as I melt against him and the asshole grins against my lips. "You'll learn, baby. I take care of what's mine even if you don't like how I do it."

Fuck.

I have no response to that as he backs away. Trying to pull myself together, I throw the towel in the hamper and grab my hairbrush. He takes it away from me, gently brushing it through my long hair.

The steam has evaporated enough that I can watch him in the blurry mirror. Tears threaten to fall as he takes care of me. It's overwhelming and I clear my throat of the lump that's forming there.

He spins me around, understanding in his eyes, his lips slowly meeting mine. The kiss is deliberate and measured, his tongue caressing mine, putting my racing heart at ease.

"Bed, sweetheart." He whispers against my lips, and I do as I'm told.

Leaving the bathroom, I head to the closet to

grab a t-shirt when strong hands wrap around my waist. He takes the shirt from my hands, tossing it on the floor. "You won't be needing that." He whispers against my ear.

My body shivers as he guides me towards the bed, pulling the covers back. Climbing on the mattress, he crawls on top of me, giving me another slow kiss that short circuits my brain.

He eases back, sliding to the other side of the bed, facing me. "Tell me about Dylan."

Knots form in my stomach and the tears are instantly back. I turn onto my side, begging him silently to not make me do this.

Thinking about my brother has always been too painful. I don't know if it's because he was so young when he died or because we actually understood each other.

Dex cups my cheek, pressing his body closer, ensuring we're touching from our chests to our toes. "Tell me about your little brother, baby."

A single sob leaves my chest. "I don't know if I can. I haven't said his name out loud since it happened."

His lips brush mine. "Say his name."

The dam breaks and I can't control my emotions any longer. My entire body shakes uncontrollably as I lean into his chest and relive the images of him lying lifeless on the floor. The worst night of my life comes back full force and I let it consume me.

We stay like this for a while. Dex holding me as

I let everything out.

My eyes finally run dry, the sobbing turns into annoying hiccups, and I pull my head from his chest. He smiles sadly, wiping away the wet trails running down my cheeks. "Say his name, Savannah."

Diving deep into myself, looking for some kind of courage, I manage to speak. "D-Dylan."

Dex's pride hits me in the chest as he wraps me in a hug, kissing the top of my head.

Feeding off his emotions, I continue. "H-he was fourteen."

He nods because he already knew that part.

"Dex, I need you to understand something." I don't wait for his response. "I had a loving family growing up. Sure, my parents both had tempers, but it was rarely directed at us. Even with everything I could've asked for, I always had dark thoughts. A part of me was always angry and volatile. I wanted to hurt people. The ones who deserved it. I could go from smiling to violent in a split second. My mom was concerned, and I think it's why she was worried about the fighting. My dad wanted me to embrace it. Even though I was going to college, I think a part of him wanted me to take over the business one day. He kept a lot of his dealings quiet, but I know for a fact he didn't want Colin to take over."

Dex sighs. "You're right. When we interrogated some of his men, we learned he was shutting Colin out. Your dad wanted you to have schooling, but his end goal was to have you and Dylan run things when he stepped down."

Now that my suspicions are confirmed, I finally understand why he wanted me and Dylan dead too. "That motherfucker."

He tucks a strand of hair behind my ear. "Tell me more about these dark thoughts of yours and what they have to do with Dylan."

"Dylan was the same way. He was so mad all the time, and I recognized myself in him. After I told him he's not alone, our relationship changed. Yeah, we still had our sibling spats, but he was different with me. He'd always apologize and actually talk to me. Even with our age difference, he was my best friend. I couldn't control my own emotions, but I guided him to control his. I loved my parents and losing them broke me. But losing Dylan? It almost killed me, Dex. I've been fighting to leave this world for the past two years, but something won't let me do it."

He grips the back of my neck, crushing his lips to mine. He doesn't let me breathe or think, just takes everything I have to give and still demands more. While my mind screams for me to push away and save myself, my body clings to him, matching his demanding pace.

He rips himself away, his pupils dilated with lust and anger. "I'm a fucking idiot, Savannah. I knew you were miserable with grief, but I didn't know you were ready to check out on me. I was trying to be patient and let you come to me, but I couldn't take it anymore. I had to make my move. I should've done it sooner. I'm so fucking sorry, baby. If I would've known-"

Pressing my fingers to his lips, I silence him. "I wasn't ready for you yet. You couldn't save me then, but you're helping me now. Just being here and hearing me, you're making a difference."

He sighs, leaning into me until our foreheads are touching. "Sorry I interrupted you. I want you to keep going if you can."

I nod. "Do you know what kills me the most? After seeing my brother and mother lying on the floor dead, my father's eyes told me to run. And I did. I fucking ran until I couldn't run anymore. Why didn't I stay and fight?"

Dex shakes his head. "You couldn't have won, baby. From what I've read, he had two guys with him." I nod in confirmation. "You're tiny without proper training. They would've killed you. You did the right thing. Running isn't a weakness, it's self-preservation. Don't feel guilty about wanting to live."

His words make sense, but it doesn't soothe the guilt I have. Maybe with time I can make peace with my decision.

"This is a heavy topic. I'm proud of you, baby. Did it help to talk about it?"

"Yeah, but can we talk about it more some other time? I need a break and I'm tired." I yawn, proving my point.

He chuckles, tucking me against his chest.

"Sleep, little chaos. We have plans tomorrow."

Chapter Thirteen

Declan

We're on our way to Jase and Rage's house.

Savannah is staring out the window, lost in thought.

She asked where we were going, and I told her to my boss's house.

After last night's talk, I realized she has a lot of pent-up rage, and she needs an outlet. Where I thought losing her family was the root cause, she explained it's been simmering since she was a teenager.

That gave me an idea.

Before she woke up, I called Jase and filled him in. I suggested she go on a job with us. She's killed two men, pieces of shit no doubt, with no remorse. She doesn't have a conscience eating her alive with guilt for killing someone who deserves it.

He was skeptical at first but told me to bring her over so he could talk to her.

Pulling into the driveway, she starts fidgeting with her hands in her lap.

"Hey." She turns towards me, and I give her a reassuring smile. "Don't be nervous. I don't particularly care for the human race, but these people are solid. They're friends and I trust them with my life."

She nods and I get out of the truck, going to her side. Opening the door, I help her out, pinning her against me. "You can trust them, Savannah."

"I trust *you*. Is that good enough for now?"

Her words settle in my chest, soothing any worry I had about today. Leaning down, I kiss her slowly and she melts against me, making me feel like a fucking king.

We approach the house and I open the front door, guiding Savannah through the threshold. She's hesitant as I lead the way, stopping at the voices coming from the kitchen.

Shit.

"Don't be upset with me, killer." Jase says and I can only imagine the look Rage is giving him right now.

"We don't bring in strangers!" Rage counters and Savannah stiffens beside me.

I try to lead her to another room to escape the conversation, but she doesn't move.

"I want to hear." She whispers.

Looking to the ceiling, I pray for anyone to make this shit go in a different direction. I don't need Savannah feeling self-conscious or unwanted.

I should've fucking knocked.

"This is a special circumstance, baby. Dex wants Savannah to come along and see how she reacts. Who better to show her the ropes than a sexy, bad-ass killer like you?" Damn. Jase is laying it on thick.

Not really. He sees Rage exactly how he describes her and where I used to find it amusing,

I find Savannah's gaze and realize it's not funny after all. It's the truth.

"Nice save, asshole." Rage quips and I can't help but grin.

"I'm serious. You're brave and a total savage, Rage. I trust you with my life and theirs."

"Damn you, sweet bastard. Why is this so important to him?" Rage asks.

"Who are you to me? Does that answer your question?" He responds.

"Oh shit!" She squeals.

Jase chuckles and I feel Savannah's gaze on me. He isn't wrong, I realized it last night, but it's a conversation for a later time. Even if today goes south, she's still mine and I will give my life to protect her at all costs.

"I get it now. Oh my God! Maybe I should be her friend! Ew, I don't like people though."

He chuckles again. "She's different, killer. She's one of us, now. Will you be nice to her?"

"I'll try. She probably needs a girl to help her adjust. Having a psycho hitman obsessed with you is really exhausting sometimes."

"Oh really?" He questions playfully.

"Um, just kidding?" Rage back tracks and Savannah snorts.

I squeeze her hand and she looks at me, smiling. "She's different." She whispers.

"You have no idea." I warn with a smirk.

"Uh huh." Jase counters.

"Since I'm going to be a good girl and try to

make a friend, do I get a reward?" Rage sounds so innocent and I'm cracking up on the inside.

"Mmm, what kind of reward, little killer?"

"You and me. No contact with the outside world. Orgasms for days."

"Fuck. I can arrange that."

"Thank you, Daddy."

Fuck me.

If they start fucking in the kitchen, we're leaving.

"Damnit Rage. Now I'm hard." Jase groans.

Gripping Savannah's hand, I pull her towards the kitchen. "We don't need to see all that boss man." I announce as we enter the room.

"Ever heard of knocking, Archer?" Jase snaps and I chuckle as he moves behind the kitchen island.

"Dex never knocks." Rage says as she approaches Savannah, holding out her hand.

Savannah straightens, gripping her hand firmly. "Just to clear the air, I don't need you to be my friend. I'm not a stray puppy."

I look to Jase as he scowls at me, and I hide a grin behind my hand.

Rage claps and turns to him. "I like her! She's welcome to kill people with us."

Savannah's wide eyes meet mine and I want to choke Rage.

Pulling her close, I explain. "After we talked last night, I thought you could go on a job with us and see what you think. We're taking out a sex trafficker downtown. He's responsible for the disappearance of dozens of teenage girls."

"You want me to kill someone?" She asks.

I shrug. "If you want to. He'll have security, but Jase and Rage have checked them out. Just a few guys who think they're big shit because they have a gun on their side."

She looks at the other two before her eyes settle on me. "What if I can't?"

Leaning in close, I kiss her softly. "I'll put you in a vest and you'll stay glued to my side. If it's too much, Rage can take you outside. This is a quick job and the three of us will protect you no matter what you decide. Either way, you'll see what I do for a living."

She smirks. "Other than stalking me?"

Rage cackles beside Jase. "Welcome to the club! Hitman stalkers are where it's at."

Savannah laughs too and I'm still surprised by the sound, only hearing it a couple of times since I've known her. "Do I get a gun?"

Jase's eyebrows shoot to his hairline, looking to me.

"Hey bossman, over here. I may be rusty from not shooting in a while, but my dad taught me." Savannah sasses and I can't deny my cock hardening at her smart-ass mouth.

His eyes soften. "What caliber do you want?"

"Nine-millimeter." That's all she says before Rage drags her from my embrace, and they head upstairs whispering the entire way.

"What have we done?" Jase groans and I chuckle.

As long as my girl is happy and safe, by my side, I'll deal with it all.

Chapter Fourteen

Savannah

This damn bullet proof vest fits like a corset.

The lack of oxygen my lungs are getting will kill me before a bullet.

Rage took me upstairs so she could fit me for a vest and she's not so bad. I actually kind of like her.

Okay, I really like her.

She's intense and her social skills are awkward, but my instincts tell me she's been through some shit.

Like me.

I'm not that great with people either. Two years of staying to yourself will do that. I don't know Rage's story and I won't pry. Maybe we *can* be friends and I'll find out.

Staring into the full-length mirror, I'm awkwardly trying to loosen the side straps on this damn thing. My eyes collide with gorgeous baby blues in the reflection and my breath hitches.

My gaze roams down his body and memories from last night flash through my mind. I catch sight of his large hands, remembering how they felt all over my body. His tongue trails across his bottom lip and my attention snaps to the seductive movement, my thighs clenching as my heart beats faster.

His full lips tug upward and when I meet his eyes again, my face heats with embarrassment.

He knows exactly what I'm thinking about.

He saunters toward me, his expression darkening.

He doesn't stop until his chest presses against my back. Bringing his lips to my ear, he whispers, "What are you thinking about, little chaos?"

His warm breath caresses the shell of my ear and my body shudders. "This vest is too tight." I lie.

He reaches for the straps on the side, adjusting the Velcro so I can breathe. One hand roams underneath, squeezing my breast and I gasp. His other hand trails down my torso, not stopping until he's cupping my pussy through my jeans.

My head falls back against his chest and a moan escapes my lips as he trails kisses down my neck. My hips grind into his hand, desperate for some kind of friction. His cock hardens at my back as he grinds against me, groaning into my neck. The vibration causes goosebumps to erupt across my skin.

"Dex, make me come." I whimper, and our eyes lock again in the mirror's reflection.

"Keep your eyes on me." He demands, sliding his hand inside my jeans, finding my aching clit, swollen and pulsing.

My entire body jolts, and I curse as he circles it slowly. "More."

His other hand leaves my breast, gripping my chin and turning my face to the side. Warm lips crash to mine, devouring me as his finger applies more pressure, moving faster.

"You're so fucking responsive to my touch. Come on my hand, baby. I want to lick you off my fingers." He groans against my mouth and his words have my pussy contracting, my lower belly coiling tightly.

His tongue pushes deeper as I grind against his finger until I explode, his kiss muffling my scream of pleasure. My legs threaten to buckle, but he holds me possessively against him with one arm. Removing his hand from between my legs, I watch in the mirror as he sucks his finger clean, closing his eyes like I'm the best thing he's ever tasted.

He grips the straps of my vest. "We're bringing this home. I want to fuck you while you're wearing nothing but this."

I'm panting already, but the anticipation of having his cock inside me again overrides the ache I have from last night.

He spins me around, all playfulness gone. "Stay by me at all times today."

Nodding in agreement, I try to take a step back.

He grips my waist, holding me in place. "I mean it, Savannah. Don't leave my side unless it's too much and Rage will get you out."

"You're so bossy." I sass, not liking the worry on his face.

This was his idea and I know his intentions are genuine. He thinks killing people will help me.

It might.

I've liked it so far.

He's giving me an out if I can't handle it, but the

way I felt after killing those other two bastards, I'm not worried.

"Savannah." He warns and I grin, still getting used to the feeling.

"I'll stay by you, Archer. Now, come on before the other two come looking for us."

He leans down, stealing another quick kiss, leaving me breathless before taking my hand, leading me downstairs.

"You ready, newbie?" Rage asks and I flip her off.

They all chuckle as we head outside, climbing into Jase's truck. He turns in his seat, handing me a black and silver nine-millimeter. She's a beauty. I remove the magazine, checking that it's full. Popping it back in, I rack it to put one in the chamber and turn the safety on.

If sixteen bullets can't get the job done, then I'm meant to die today.

A large, abandoned warehouse comes into view, but Jase pulls off the road before we get there.

"Shouldn't we be wearing black or something?" I ask, immediately rolling my eyes at the dumb question.

Dex turns to me. "That's for nighttime killing, baby. During the day, we want to look normal, so no one suspects us."

Well, that makes sense.

Jase and Rage exit the truck, but Dex wraps his hand around my throat, pulling me closer. "By me."

"Yes, sir." I breathe, his fingers flexing at my response.

"Careful, little chaos." He growls before kissing me hard and fast, nipping my bottom lip as he pulls away.

My heart is racing from his touch, my stomach churning with nerves. I have no idea what the fuck I'm about to walk into, but I trust Dex.

It may be murder in some people's eyes, but we see it as retribution.

In my case, a way of healing, a kind of therapy.

He exits the truck, and I turn the safety off on my gun. Before I can reach for the handle on the door, it opens and he grips my hand, pulling me forward. Turning to head towards the others, he slaps my ass and I stifle a retort.

Sending him a death glare, he smiles proudly as he checks his own gun before sliding it in the waistband of his pants.

We meet Rage and Jase in an alley beside the old warehouse.

"So, ambush?" I ask, confirming the plan we discussed in the truck on the way here.

"Ambush." They reply in unison.

My gun is already in my hand, the comfortable weight settling deep in my gut.

I'm okay with this.

The others pull out their guns, racking them, ready to take out any threat they encounter.

My index finger absorbs the coolness of the

metal slide as it presses there, away from the trigger.

"Never put your finger on the trigger unless you're ready to take the life in front of you." My father's words echo through my mind and instead of causing sadness, they give me a boost of confidence.

We walk cautiously down the alleyway, checking our surroundings, before reaching the side door of the building.

Some security.

There's no one guarding the door.

Rolling my eyes, I glance at Dex, smirking like he knows what I'm thinking. "Ready?" He asks.

"Ready." I nod.

Rage and I take our positions at the side of the door. Jase checks the knob and it's unlocked. It's a fucking chore to stay focused and not roll my eyes again.

He jerks the door open, Dex going inside first. My anxiety spikes.

I don't like him going in first.

Jase quickly follows and turns back a few seconds later whispering, "Clear".

We follow behind the guys, guns raised, our bodies taut. We're all on high alert as we weave through aisles of old, rusted racks, trying to find the asshole we're here for.

"What the fuck are you doing in here? I pay you to guard the fucking door, you idiot!" A man yells and all our heads swing towards the voice.

"Bingo!" Rage whispers and we peek through one of the racks, watching as a big guy eating a bag of chips comes towards us.

"And stop eating all the time. How the fuck are you supposed to protect this place if your hands are always full of food?" The voice yells again.

Dick.

Maybe he's comfort eating because he works for an asshole like you.

What am I saying?

Potato chip guy is bad, and he will have to die, too.

We'll kill him last so he can enjoy his snack.

We squat down as he passes and watch as he exits the building. As I glance back to where the voice was yelling, I see him.

Victor Jones.

He's a known trafficker and I felt nauseous when Jase showed me his picture. He's responsible for over thirty disappearances in the city and surrounding areas. He thinks he's untouchable because half the police department is in his pocket.

Today, he will be touched. With multiple bullets.

I'll admit, I was concerned how I'd react to this situation. The two guys I killed were trying to hurt me. To walk up and kill someone I'd never met bothered me a little.

Once Jase filled me in on Victor, my view changed.

There are at least thirty families out there

whose lives were ruined. They've lost their daughters to this man. He's solely responsible for their misery and suffering. Once that thought settled in, I was ready to make him bleed.

He's sitting at a desk, counting a shit ton of money. Two guards stand on either side of him, another one looming behind his chair. There's another guy stacking the cash in a brief case at a table beside the desk.

We hold our position, making sure they're all accounted for.

Jase drops his hand, our eyes tracking the motion, waiting for the signal. His fingers straighten, giving us the go ahead.

We rise to our feet, making our presence known as we dart out from behind the racks. Each of us pick a target, Rage alternating her gun between hers and the odd fifth guy.

"Drop your weapons." Jase barks and all eyes swing to us.

Drawing their guns, they all start yelling, and we're in a standoff.

I don't miss Dex inching closer, his body shielding mine. I only have a clear line of sight to my target. Out of the corner of my eye, Jase does the same to Rage.

She huffs in annoyance. Meeting her gaze, she winks with a grin, mouthing, "Men".

The girl really is a nut, but I'm liking her more and more.

My target shifts, locking eyes with me and I

grin, the action noticeably unnerving him. Sweat forms on his forehead as he shifts on his feet. He's probably in his early thirties, already sporting a combover and ridiculous suspenders are holding up his pants.

Who the hell wears suspenders anymore?

"Who the fuck are you?" Victor demands and I try to move around Dex so I can see, but a deep growl rumbles in his chest, effectively keeping me behind him.

"Death." Dex grits out.

Victor laughs. "I suppose you came to meet yours."

"We need to spread out." Rage whispers. "We're the fucking targets now."

"No." Dex and Jase say at the same time.

"Boys, take care of them." Victor barks, sitting back in his chair.

My target cocks his gun, stepping away from the desk, aiming it at my chest.

Before I can blink, a gun fires, a hole appearing in his forehead.

Dex drew the first blood.

He pushes me back, Rage grabbing my wrist, pulling me down to the ground.

As chaos erupts around us, we roll under a rack, lying on our stomachs. I quickly aim for the one firing at Dex, hitting him in the chest. He falls to the ground, pressing a hand to his wound while gasping for air. Dex and Jase are both behind beams, firing and dodging bullets simultaneously.

Jase hits the guy filling the briefcase, blood instantly gushing from his torso.

The door swings open and in comes chip guy, but before he has time to process the scene, Rage rolls to her back, shooting him in the titty. He falls to the ground, howling in pain, but I ignore him, turning back to cover the guys.

Victor cowers under his desk, and I watch closely as his hand rises blindly, grabbing the cash from the top. Theres one guy left other than Victor and the son-of-a-bitch is hiding behind the wall, shooting around the corner, bullets flying in every direction.

But my focus is on Victor.

The longer I watch him reach for the cash with a fucking bloodbath going on around him, the more pissed I get.

Crawling out from underneath the rack, Rage hisses my name, but I ignore her. Dragging my body across the floor on my forearms, I avoid the gunfire as I reach the desk. Pulling my pocketknife from my jeans, I wait patiently until Victor's hand reappears.

Flicking my blade open, his hand connects with the desk. I rise quickly, stabbing him through the top of his hand, pinning it to the wooden top. Victor roars in pain, reaching for the knife to pull it out.

The gunfire stops, the guy behind the wall effectively taken out by Jase or Dex. Before I can turn to check, Victor jumps from the ground, punching me in the face. I stumble backwards, the gun falling from my other hand, sliding across the floor.

My jaw throbs and my vision blurs. A growl comes from above me before a series of gunshots puts Victor to sleep permanently.

Everything is silent for a moment before I'm pulled into strong arms. "Are you okay?" Dex asks, scanning my face.

"Yeah." I reply and it hurts like a bitch.

"You and Rage take her to the truck, and I'll make sure none of them are still breathing. Rage text cleanup for me, baby."

In my peripheral vision, I see Jase hug Rage, giving her a quick kiss as they share a secret smile. Dex heads for the door, with me in his arms, his jaw clenched so tightly he may chip his beautiful teeth.

As we reach the truck, he opens the back door, gently sitting me in the seat. He doesn't say a word as he walks to the other side, climbing inside.

"Dex, are you-"

He cuts me off. "Savannah, don't. I told you to stay by me and you decide to dive into gunfire blindly to stab the motherfucker in the hand."

Rage joins us as my temper flares. "He was driving me crazy, reaching for the money while all his men were dying around him!"

"He fucking hit you!" He shouts and I lean back against my seat, surprised.

"Let's just all take a moment to calm down."

Rage says softly.

"Fuck this! He wanted me to come and kill people and now he's mad because I did. Throwing a fucking tantrum like a child. If I was supposed to hide under that rack, then there was no point in me coming."

In the next moment, I'm pulled down into the seat, Dex looming over me with a dangerous look in his eyes. "He. Fucking. Hit. You." He seethes and the darkness in his eyes sets my body on fire.

Gripping his shirt, I pull him down on top of me, crashing our lips together. It hurts like a motherfucker, but I won't stop. He growls into my mouth, his hands fisting my hair, angling my head to deepen the kiss. Shoving my hands under his vest and shirt, I drag my nails down his torso.

A door opens, but he doesn't pull away and neither do I. We're completely lost in each other, the adrenaline still coursing through our bodies.

"Uh, everybody okay?" Jase asks awkwardly and Rage laughs.

He cranks the truck, and we drive off as Dex finally pulls away. My body rises to chase him, but he holds me in place. He stares at my mouth, his forehead creasing with concern. If it looks half as bad as it feels, I'm not very cute right now.

"I'm sorry I yelled at you, baby." He leans down, kissing the corner of my mouth and I flinch from the sting of pain.

"It's okay, it was in the heat of the moment. But if you do it again, I'll stab you." I realize then I don't have my knife and it pisses me off. "I need a new knife."

Dex grins as he leans back in his seat, pulling me into his side. "I got you, little savage."

Chapter Fifteen

Declan

I wish I could bring Victor back to life just to kill his ass again, slowly.

When I finally shot the bastard who was hiding behind the wall, I was relieved. The entire time I was terrified a stray bullet would hit one of us, especially Savannah.

As he hit the ground, I turned just as Victor sucker punched her in the face.

I saw red.

I've never felt so fucking murderous in my life.

I emptied my clip into his chest without blinking.

It did nothing to calm the rage inside me.

Once we got in the truck, I lost my temper and now I feel like a piece of shit. Even though I was pissed she put herself in a vulnerable position, it was my fault.

I thought today would help her, but I shouldn't have introduced her to my life with an ambush. I didn't think much of it because Jase, Rage and I live for this shit. It's an adrenaline rush and we cover each other easily while killing assholes like Victor.

The ones who *deserve* it.

I should've eased Savannah into this.

There's always a risk when we do a job. Instead of a strategically planned hit, sometimes we have to go in and take out everyone at once. I was fully prepared to protect her with my life, but I can't do that if she pulls the shit she did today.

On the other hand, I'm proud of her. Rage told me she killed a guy who was aiming at me. She described Savannah stabbing Victor's hand to the desk as "beautiful".

That's Rage for you.

Knowing she wasn't scared and she's willing to protect us *is* beautiful.

Speaking of beauty, the door opens and my heart sinks as my little savage comes out of the steam filled bathroom, sporting a massive purple bruise on her jaw. Her bottom lip is split, and I'm fucking pissed all over again.

The mattress dips as she sits beside me on the bed, wearing only a towel. Running my hand down my face, I try to regain my control.

Even bruised, she's the sexiest woman I've ever seen and while I'm angry, my cock hardens, desperate to be inside her after what happened today.

"I'm okay, Dex. I used to fight all the time. Contrary to what you may believe, I didn't always win."

Meeting her gaze, she watches me closely and I grin. "So, you've had a few shiners, little chaos?"

She tries to smile, but winces in pain. "I've had my fair share."

Pushing her onto her back, I crawl over her, holding my weight on my forearms. Running my nose down the length of her throat, she smells of lavender and vanilla. I close my eyes, breathing deeply.

She's okay.

Her fingers sink into my wet hair, and I kiss her neck, her sweet taste calming me. I took a shower at my apartment while she showered here. I didn't want to leave her, but I needed to chill the fuck out. Now, I realize I didn't need time alone, I only needed her. She tugs my hair and I lift my head.

Fuck, she's gorgeous.

More than anything, I want to take her mouth, while I sink inside her and forget everything for a little while.

"Talk to me." Her sweet voice wraps around me.

"God, I want to kiss you." I groan.

"Kiss me then." She whispers and I shake my head.

"I'm not going to hurt you, baby."

Her fingers tighten in my hair. "I can take the pain."

My cock twitches at her words, tempting me. She looks disappointed as I shake my head again. "I'm going to kiss you everywhere else."

She perks up, her eyes clouding over with lust. Against my better judgement, I kiss the corner of her mouth, opposite the side of her injury. She doesn't flinch, arousal overriding any pain she may feel. Her lip's part and I carefully push my tongue inside. She whimpers and I pull back, but she shakes her head. "Don't stop."

Without another word, I pull apart the towel, my mouth trailing down her body, sucking and licking her smooth skin as she trembles beneath me. She spreads her legs instinctively as I reach her pussy, swollen and wet, needing my touch. Spreading her lips open with my fingers, I lick her from top to bottom. Her flavor bursts on my tongue and I realize I could survive off her alone.

She moans long and deep, the sound causing me to lunge forward, pushing my tongue inside her as deep as it will go. She grinds on my face, her fingers tightening in my hair. The bite of pain spurs me on, and I suck her clit into my mouth, sliding two fingers inside her tight hole.

She writhes beneath me, little noises escaping her battered mouth, and I growl at the reminder. Her pussy clenches around my fingers as I pump faster, curving them to find her sweet spot.

She screams my name and I pull my fingers free, plunging my tongue inside her again. Drinking every drop of her orgasm, I reach down, freeing my cock from my sweatpants. Squeezing the base tightly, I try my damnedest not to come from the taste of her.

Once her body relaxes, I crawl over her and she opens her eyes slowly, unfocussed, and satiated.

"Lick my lips."

Her little tongue darts out, quickly tracing my lips.

"The taste of you almost made me come in my fucking pants." I groan, running my cock through her wet slit, my piercings bumping her clit with every pass.

"I need you." She whispers, raising her hips to take me inside her.

"You want my cock, baby? You want me to fuck this tight little pussy until you can't take anymore?"

Fuck.

I'm torturing us both.

"Dex, please!" She cries, chasing my dick as I tease her.

Unable to take anymore, I notch myself at her opening, thrusting inside her until I bottom out.

We both moan at the feeling of coming together. Being inside her is like coming home.

"Savannah." Her name is a prayer on my lips.

She wraps her legs around my waist, her arms around my shoulders. I bury my face in the crook of her neck, muffling the sounds of my own pleasure against her skin. Keeping a slow pace, I fill her completely with every stroke, both our bodies trembling.

Snaking my arms underneath her, I pin her against me, rising to my knees.

"Oh!" She moans, the new position letting me sink deeper.

"Feel me possess you, Savannah. You're fucking mine." I'm unravelling and I know she senses it.

She grips my shoulders as I hold her hips, slamming her down on my cock as I thrust into her. She screams my name as I fuck her senseless, the signs of our pending orgasms creeping up on us. Her pussy clenches around me as my balls tighten, heat shooting down my spine.

"Come." I growl.

"Oh God!" She screams as I slam her hips down harder, my dick swelling just before I come.

We cling to each other, panting for air as I rotate my hips, dragging every drop of pleasure from her body. She slumps against my chest, shaking uncontrollably and I press kisses to the top of her head. I don't loosen my grip, wanting to stay like this for as long as we can.

Chapter Sixteen

Savannah

A few days have passed, the bruising finally beginning to fade from my face.

Dex has smothered me to the point I've wanted to throat punch him a few times. It's nice to be taken care of, but I don't need assistance brushing my teeth and peeing.

I've gotten plenty of sympathetic looks from customers at the diner. One lady even wrote down the domestic abuse hotline number on a napkin when she left.

The staring bothers me, as does the pity, because it's not what they think. If they only knew the circumstances surrounding my bruises, they'd look at me with fear.

"We need to train." Dex says as I join him on the couch, bowl of popcorn in hand.

"Train for what? I know how to fight."

He takes the bowl from my hand, sitting it on the coffee table. "You know how to scrap, little chaos. I want to train you how to protect yourself."

Rolling my eyes, I grab the remote, searching for a movie to watch. "I protect myself just fine."

He snatches the remote from my hand, flinging it to the floor. Balling my fists, I turn to knock the shit out of him, but his hand circles my throat, pinning me to the couch cushion.

He hovers over me, his eyes darkening. "A

surprise attack won you your first kill. Your second kill ended with you tripping over the dead guy's arm, almost being murdered by his partner. You stabbed Victor and then *he* sucker punched *you*."

My blood boils at his insults and I claw at his hand, wanting him to bleed as my temper flares. "Fuck you!"

My leg kicks out, but he dodges the blow meant for his balls. He chuckles and I want nothing more than to kick him in the face.

"You won't get the upper hand in every fight. When you can't throw a punch, you need to be able to dodge one."

What he's saying makes sense, but it still pisses me off. "You're a dick."

He releases my throat, gripping my biceps, pulling me to stand in front of him. "I'm being honest. I don't sugar coat shit, little one. I'll always be real with you."

Blowing out a breath, I nod, my offended pride taking a backseat to what I know is true. I need training. "When and where?"

"I'm taking you where we all train. Now." His hands slide around my waist, pulling me against him.

Tipping my head back, I look into his eyes as he leans down. "You're still a dick."

His lips twitch with amusement. "I'm your dick."

I grin before meeting his lips, my mind in the gutter right next to his.

Walking through the door of the training facility, I'm relieved the place is empty.

It's one thing to train with Dex, but another for people to see him put me on my ass.

I'm wearing athletic shorts and a tank top. I wanted to be comfortable, but nothing baggy to hinder my movements.

He walks across the room, tossing his gym bag on a bench before pulling out his phone. His fingers move quickly and a second later, the room fills with loud, metal music. The drums and base vibrate the floor beneath me, and the fast tempo has my blood pumping.

He grabs the back of his shirt, jerking it over his head. Tan skin peaks through the ink covering his body and I lick my lips, my mouth suddenly dry.

He's wearing a pair of black basketball shorts, hanging low on his hips, giving me a much-appreciated view of his v muscles.

My gaze slowly roams over his body until I meet his smug grin. "Are you going to be able to concentrate, little chaos?"

Deciding to play dirty too, I slowly remove my tank top, left only in my black shorts and black sports bra. His jaw clenches, and I smile in victory. "Are you?"

He clears his throat, striding towards me on the mats with determination and hunger in his eyes. He doesn't stop until we're toe to toe and my breath hitches as the back of his hand skims down my torso. "It'll be damn near impossible, but I'll try."

Goosebumps erupt across my skin as his fingers trail up my arms, not stopping until he grips the back of my neck with one hand, wrapping my ponytail around the other.

He slams his lips to mine, and I moan into his mouth, this being our first real kiss in days. My lips are still tender, but I ignore it as he devours me until nothing exists but him.

Pulling away abruptly, he lets go of my neck and ponytail, his hands moving to my chest. With a grin that screams he's about to piss me off, he pushes me backwards. "Show me what you got, *little one*." He taunts while stretching his limbs, slipping his hands into a pair of boxing gloves.

A dangerous concoction mixes like an elixir inside my veins. Adrenaline has my blood singing, eager to beat his ass after he teased the hell out of me. Lust simmers just below the surface, humming appreciation for the gorgeous male specimen in front of me. One way or another, my hands will be on him.

He bounces back and forth on his feet, priming his body for a fight. It helps with your reaction time since you're already moving.

He watches me intently as I stretch my muscles before putting on my gloves, pulling the velcro tightly with my teeth and following his lead. His eyes widen in surprise at the action.

He has no idea.

I may have fumbled when I killed that asshole at our apartment building. I may have reacted impulsively when I stabbed Victor in the hand.

But an old school fist fight? *I got this.*

As we circle each other, I'm grateful he's not treating me like I'm made of glass. I was worried he'd take it easy on me. Those worries evaporate as my legs are swept out from under me and I land on my ass.

"Keep your head in the fight, Banks!" He barks and the familiar flare of self-preservation kicks in.

Punching a fist into the mat, I jump to my feet, completely focused on my opponent. "Bring it, asshole."

He grins wickedly and before I can blink, he lunges for my midsection. Spinning to the side, his momentum carries him straight into the wall behind me.

While I smile on the inside, I keep my expression blank as he turns around, his eyes darkening, focused solely on me. "Smooth, little chaos."

He meets me on the mat again and we circle each other, waiting for the other to strike. Every few steps he jumps at me, and I retreat a step. I've been on defense so far.

It's time to come alive.

He moves to taunt me once again, but I lunge forward, my fist connecting with his jaw. His head snaps back, both surprised and impressed. "Good shot, baby. I bet you can't do it again."

Something primal surges forward at his challenge and in an instant, everything changes.

He lunges forward, his gloved fist connecting with my cheek. He doesn't use his full strength, just enough to get my attention. It knocks me off balance for a moment, but I recover quickly, punching him in the side.

The crazy bastard laughs as I keep the shots coming, his torso, his thigh, his bicep. He's the one on the defense now and the more he smiles, the more I want to pummel his perfect face. I deliver punch after punch until he's backed against the wall.

"Mercy! Mercy!" He chuckles.

My sweat slicked body straightens, and I breathe through my nose, trying to calm my rapid heart rate. He pushes off the wall slowly, his large body towering over me. He moves to kiss me, but as my eyes close, his leg kicks out, knocking me to the mat.

My eyes snap open and he's on me, ravaging my mouth like he's starving for something only I can give him. He nips my bottom lip, soothing the sting with his tongue.

He breaks away, bringing a glove to his mouth, ripping the velcro open with his teeth. He locks it in the crook of his arm, pulling it from his hand, slinging it across the room. He repeats the action with the other glove and then his lips are back on mine.

My legs spread immediately, cradling his large

frame between my thighs. He grips my wrists, pulling my arms above my head, undoing the gloves, and pulling them off.

"You have to stay focused, little one. You were on guard until I went to kiss you." He breathes against my lips.

My back arches as his mouth licks a trail across my jaw and down my throat. "That won't be a problem since I don't usually kiss people I'm fighting with."

His body tenses. "You better not be kissing anyone else, period."

Possessive ass.

I hum softly and his gaze snaps to mine, pupils blown wide. "Savannah." He warns.

He releases my wrists, my hands diving into his dark hair. "There's no one but you, Declan Archer."

A deep growl rumbles in his chest before he crashes his mouth to mine, his large hands gripping the waistband of my shorts, pulling them down my legs in one frantic move, along with my panties.

My hand trails down his slick skin, over the ridges of his torso, slipping into his shorts. His hard cock is too big to wrap my fingers around, but I give it my best effort. Stroking him firmly, he groans into my mouth, his own fingers swiping through my drenched pussy lips.

"Fuck." He groans, lifting his hips as I push down his shorts enough to free his waiting cock.

Lining himself up with my slick opening, he thrusts inside me until he's buried completely. My pussy clenches around him, still not used to his size and I whimper into his chest.

His hand snakes around my throat, tilting my head back until our eyes lock. We're suspended in time, our bodies joined together, our breathing in sync with each other.

The intensity is almost too much, but I don't look away. I want this fierce connection. More importantly, I want it with *him*.

"Savannah." He whispers, as if he senses my thoughts.

My eyes burn as I hold back the emotion filling my chest. It's too soon for all of this, but it's happening, and I can't stop it.

Declan Archer blew into my life like a tornado and all I can do is hang on for the ride and see where I land.

Grinding my hips against him, a low moan escapes my lips, and he starts to move. "Oh my God."

He pulls out until just the tip remains inside me. Lifting my hips, I chase his touch, never wanting anything as much as I want him.

He leans down, taking my mouth in a brutal kiss. Our tongues battle each other as he slams inside me, swallowing my scream.

Sweet Dex has left the room, replaced with a ruthless predator, hell bent on making me bend to his will.

While we fought just a few minutes ago, I surrender to him now.

My body is his.

And if I'm not careful, my heart will be too.

Chapter Seventeen

Declan

I'm so fucked.

Watching her, she got under my skin.

Speaking to her, she stole my heart.

Every time I take her body, she takes a piece of my fucking soul.

Pride like I've never felt swelled inside me as I let her beat my ass.

She doesn't need to know that part.

While she appears small and fragile, a fire grows inside Savannah and she's unstoppable now.

That first punch to my jaw caught me off guard, but the twinkle in her eyes told me all I needed to know.

She's a fighter.

And I'll gladly take every blow she gives to see that fucking fire grow.

"Dex, I-I'm going to come." She whimpers and I groan as her tight pussy walls choke my cock.

"Strangle my cock with your tight little cunt, baby."

She moans loudly and that familiar sensation tingles down my spine. My balls tighten and I slam into her over and over, slightly concerned I may fuck her through the mat.

Worry fades as her inner walls clamp down around me, screaming my name as her orgasm tears through her. Gripping her hips with bruising force, I chase my own release, finding it three thrusts later.

Driving as deep as I can, I fill her with every drop of cum my cock is willing to give. Collapsing on top of her, my forearms catch most of my weight as I bury my face in her neck.

Even after fighting and fucking, my girl still smells like lavender and vanilla. Breathing deeply, I fill my lungs with her soothing scent.

"Not trying to give you a big head, but you're really good at that." She says, running her nails along my scalp.

I'm paralyzed by her touch, but as her words sink in, I chuckle. "It's all you, little chaos."

She scoffs, tugging my hair playfully. "I was literally a virgin a few days ago. It's not me."

Meeting her eyes, she looks unsure. "It doesn't matter if you were a virgin. Your sweet little pussy consumes me. I want you all the time. I want to live inside you, feel the warmth of your body wrapped around me every second of the day."

She gasps at my words, the doubt from a few moments ago disappearing completely. "That was really sweet in a dirty sort of way."

I chuckle. "You bring out the best in me."

Rising to my knees, I pull up my shorts, reaching for her once I'm decent. She takes my hands and I help her up, pulling her panties and shorts back into place.

A thought pops into my head, a little too late, but it still needs to be addressed. "Are you on birth control, little one?"

"Yeah." She responds, straightening her sports bra.

Damn. I was so consumed with getting inside her, I didn't play with her tits.

Later.

"I have the implant. You never know what curveballs life will throw at you." She winks.

Brat.

Wrapping my arms around her waist, I pull her against me. "I'm a curveball, baby?"

"You're something alright." She grins, breaking free from my hold.

Strutting her sexy ass across the mat, she grabs our shit, heading towards the door. "Come on, curveball. I'm starving and I need a shower."

We've trained hard over the past week, Savannah giving it everything she's got.

My girl has transformed into a fucking weapon and it's beautiful.

She's got the best of me a few times and while it makes me proud, it also makes me hard. Usually, by the end of our sessions, she's naked with either my head or my cock between her legs.

Waking up next to her every morning is something I'll never deserve, but I'll never let her go regardless.

She's mine and the sooner I kill Colin, the quicker we can start our lives together.

My phone rings and I pull it from my pocket to

see its Jase. "Yeah?"

"Word on the street is Colin knows Savannah is here." My body tenses at his grave tone.

"How?" I grit out.

"His guys must have spotted her at the diner."

Fuck!

"I'm not letting her go back there."

"Yeah, let me know how that goes." He replies, amusement in his voice.

My jaw clenches. "What the fuck do you suggest?"

He chuckles. "Don't demand she quit her job, Dex. She'll get pissed, you will too and nothing good will come of it. *Talk* to her about it."

"Fine." I snap and end the call.

Jase's warning weighed heavily on my mind until I decided to take matters into my own hands.

While Savannah was at work today, I drove a couple of towns over, stopping by a jewelry store. Looking inside every glass case in the damn place, I searched for something fitting my little chaos.

Just as I'm about to give up and leave for another store, something catches my eye.

A necklace.

The charm is eight separate arrows pointing in different directions. The stems of the arrows all meet in the middle, joined together by a black stone.

The symbol of chaos.

Fucking perfect.

The only reason I know that is because symbols are something I've always been interested in. My body is covered in ink, and I research thoroughly before every tattoo.

After paying for the necklace, I sent Jase a text before meeting him at the office.

I explained my idea and he smirked, calling me a "sneaky bastard".

With his help we altered the charm, placing a tracker on the backside of the stone. It couldn't be seen which I was thankful for. Against my better judgment, I'll have to keep the tracking device a secret. I don't want her thinking I'm infringing on her privacy, or I don't trust her to take care of herself.

I'm just a protective motherfucker when it comes to my girl and her safety will always come first.

She deserves nice things and once I kill Colin, I'll hand her the world on a silver platter. With that being said, it doesn't mean I can't spoil my girl for selfish reasons, too.

A knock on my front door grabs my attention and I set the jewelry box down on the counter.

Opening the door, I'm met by a gorgeous, yet exhausted, Savannah. She strolls inside without saying a word as I close the door behind us.

She turns to face me, worrying her bottom lip and I'm instantly on edge. "What's wrong?" I demand.

She exhales shakily. "Nothing. I just...I really

missed you today."

I sigh with relief, pulling her into my arms. "Do you not normally miss me?" She huffs a breath against my chest, and I pull back, lifting her chin with my finger until our eyes meet.

"I do. Today was worse. I don't know what I'm trying to say. I sound like a damn weirdo." She rambles and I lean down, silencing her with a kiss.

She fists the front of my shirt and I deepen the kiss, losing myself in her warmth and sweet flavor. Lifting her by the backs of her thighs, she wraps her legs around my waist as I spin us towards the wall, pinning her against it.

"Fuck, I miss you every second you're out of my sight." I whisper against her lips, and she moans, gripping the hair at the nape of my neck.

She whimpers and my mind chooses that moment to remind me of the necklace. Pulling away, she chases me and damn if I don't dive back in, taking another hit of my addiction.

My obsession.

We stay like this, lost in each other, trying desperately to make up for the time we were apart.

Her head falls back against the wall as I lick a trail across her jawline. Reaching her soft earlobe, I nip the sensitive skin, whispering, "I got you something."

Her eyes snap open. "You got me a surprise?"

"Yep." I smirk.

She pats my chest with both hands, squirming for me to put her down. "What is it? Where is it?"

She's so fucking excited and my chest tightens, wanting to bottle this energy for when she has those hard days.

"Sit." I say, pointing towards the couch.

She obeys, skipping over and plopping down on the cushion.

Grabbing the box off the counter, I head towards the couch, Savannah bouncing like a kid on Christmas morning. Sitting beside her, I hand her the box, watching her face as she opens it.

She gasps, her smile fading, and I immediately grip her chin, searching her eyes. They're filled with tears, her bottom lip quivering.

"Hey." I whisper, cupping her cheek in my palm.

The tears fall and she hiccups. "I was expecting chocolate or a book."

I grin, pulling the necklace from the box. "Do you like it?"

She sniffs. "It's the most beautiful thing I've ever seen." She slowly turns to the side, lifting her hair. Clasping the silver chain around her neck, she drops her hair, facing me once again.

"Do you know what the symbol means?" I ask.

She shakes her head.

"It's the symbol for chaos." I smile and she laughs, wrapping her arms around my neck.

"Thank you, Dex. It's gorgeous."

"Not as gorgeous as you, little one."

Climbing onto my lap, she kisses me slowly, and I keep the moment gentle, knowing she needs it. Ten minutes ago, we were a frenzy of tongues and hands. Now, I'm embracing every moment of this slow torture.

"Is this okay?" She asks, almost like she senses my thoughts.

"You need firmness when you're fiery and softness when you're vulnerable. I'll always take care of you."

She gives me a watery smile before nuzzling her face in the crook of my neck. Sliding my hand under her shirt, my fingers trail up and down her spine.

"I need a shower." She whispers.

"Me too. Come on, we'll shower together and conserve water."

"Perv." She swats my chest.

Standing from the couch, she squeals as I take her with me, carrying her into the bathroom. Stripping her clothes off, I quickly remove mine, gripping her hand to pull her in with me.

"Wait. I need to take my necklace off."

My body tenses. "No." The tracker is waterproof, and the thought of her taking it off *really* fucking bothers me.

"Why?" She asks.

"Never take this necklace off. Promise me, Savannah."

"Um, is this some kind of territorial thing that guys do?

"Yeah, baby. I want to see my jewelry on you at all times." She's mine and not only will this necklace help me keep her safe, but it also claims her as mine.

"I promise I'll never take it off."

Chapter Eighteen

Savannah

After our shower, we head to my apartment so I can get my laundry together.

Once inside, I sit on the couch, deciding it can wait. I'm exhausted and I'd rather spend my time learning more about Dex. The closer we get, the more I want to know about his past. "Tell me what life was like for you before you met Charles."

He relaxes into the cushions, brushing his hand down his face. "I don't know if you want to hear this, little chaos."

I scoot closer, gripping his hand with both of mine. "I want to know everything about you, Declan Archer."

He sighs heavily. "My mother had me when she was sixteen. I never knew my real father because he bailed when he found out she was pregnant. My grandparents took care of me for the most part because she couldn't be bothered with me. I remember her always telling them she was still young, and she needed to live her life. After she graduated high school, she left, and I never saw her again. They did what they had to do to raise me, but there wasn't any love in their house."

Squeezing his hand with reassurance, I urge him to continue.

"They had my mother late in life. Because they were elderly and didn't really give a fuck about me,

I had free reign to do whatever I wanted. I hung out with a rough crowd and got into a lot of trouble. Some guys told me about an underground fight ring, so I checked it out." He closes his eyes for a moment. "I was fifteen years old, and these guys beat my ass like a grown man. They didn't give a fuck. I can't blame them though. It was my choice to get involved. I had anger issues from my father not being around and then my mother leaving. I liked the challenge. I liked the pain. I craved it. It made me feel something."

Silently, I listen as Dex tells me about his loveless childhood and my heart aches for the little boy who no one cared about. His grandparents gave him the essentials to live, but beyond that he was alone.

"One of the guys paid the entry fee for my first few fights, but after that, I needed quick cash. I started pickpocketing people to get what I needed. I did that for over a year, supporting my own version of therapy. After a fight, I was focused, but it never lasted long. I always needed more, so I kept stealing which led to breaking into houses a few times. I didn't like busting into people's homes, it was too risky. I didn't need the cops on my ass, so I went back to what was easiest. My last victim was Charles, and you know how that went."

"Were you not in school?" I ask.

He shakes his head. "All I did was fight, so I dropped out when I was fourteen. My grandparents didn't even notice for a while because I was gone all the time."

"Where are your grandparents now?"

"Dead. When I met Charles, I never went back home. He kept tabs on them though. He came to me when I was eighteen and told me they died when their house caught on fire." He sighs. "According to Charles, it was electrical."

His dull eyes stare into the distance and I can't take it. Climbing onto his lap, I cradle his head against my chest. "I'm sorry you were alone so long."

He kisses the valley between my breasts, pulling away to look at me. "My family was shit, but I'm not alone anymore. I have you."

Liking the sound of that, I smile. "Yeah, you do."

Gripping the back of my neck, he pulls me into a kiss. It's soul crushing, stealing the breath from my lungs. It's like I'm in an alternate universe when he kisses me. Everything disappears but the two of us.

My life has changed dramatically since meeting Dex. His presence shifted the heavy weight I carried in my heart. It was a battle. Wanting to let him in, but needing to keep him at a distance, away from danger.

Ironically, the thing that brought me back to life was death.

And he didn't judge me.

He was proud of me for protecting myself.

He was there to help when I couldn't handle it

on my own.

He's building me up and helping me be the person I want to be.

He breaks away, both of us panting. "There will never be anyone but you, little chaos. Neither of us will ever be alone again." His finger traces the charm on my necklace, his eyes distant.

"Hey, what is it?" I ask, concern clawing at my chest.

His eyes snap to mine. "I need to talk to you about something."

I nod. "Okay."

"I got a call from Jase today. Word is Colin knows you're here in town."

His words settle like a concrete block, and it feels like my heart stops beating. "How?" I choke out.

He wraps his arms around me, drawing soothing circles on my back with his fingers, but it does little to comfort me.

"Jase thinks his guys saw you at the diner. You don't go anywhere else, so it makes sense."

"I need my job. It isn't much, but it pays the bills."

He takes my hands in his, his gaze unwavering. "I have more money than I can spend, baby. Let me take care of you."

My eyes widen. "No! I'm not some helpless girl who needs a man to take care of her." Jumping off his lap, I pace the room.

He stands immediately, tugging me into his

arms. "I know you're independent, Savannah. I would never take that away from you. I'm trying to keep you safe. Once all of this is over, we can go anywhere, buy a house. You can get a new job if you want. But right now, your safety comes first."

Slumping against his body, I know everything he's saying makes sense, but one detail sticks out in my mind. "You want us to live together?"

He chuckles. "That's what you took away from what I just said? Yeah, baby. We basically live together now."

"Oh." That's true. We've been inseparable other than when I go to work.

"I'm not trying to keep you prisoner. I only want you safe."

His concern is genuine. While I don't want to depend on anyone for anything, in this instance, I need help.

He senses my inner turmoil, brushing his thumb across my bottom lip. "You know I buy better snacks anyway." He smiles, waggling his eyebrows.

"You're an idiot." I laugh. "Fine. But when this is over, I'll be going back to work."

He kisses me soundly, his tongue showing his gratitude. "Let's watch a movie. Pick something out and I'll pop us some popcorn."

I grimace. "We don't have any more popcorn."

His jaw drops. "The fuck?"

Rolling my eyes, I grab the remote, laying back on the couch. "The store is literally ten minutes from here."

He perks up. "Come on."

"But I'm already comfortable." I whine.

His brows furrow. "I'm not leaving you here by yourself."

He's still tense about Colin being closer than we thought, but he doesn't know where I live. "I'll be fine. I'll lock up when you leave."

He pulls me into his arms, whispering against my ear. "Don't open the door for anyone but me."

Lifting on my toes, I kiss him on the cheek. "10-4. I can kick your ass, so I'll be fine."

He grins. "I'm hard just thinking about it."

Pushing him towards the door, his face grows serious. "Lock the door. Don't go outside."

With a sweet smile, I flip him off and he shakes his head as the door closes.

Heading into the kitchen, I put away the dishes from the drainer. Wiping down the counters, I clean the small place to keep myself busy. Once I'm finished, I turn on the water to wash my hands.

A faint, high pitched cry catches my attention as I turn off the faucet.

Moving towards the door, I hold my breath in the silence when I hear it again. It sounds like a hurt animal, and I hurry to unlock the door.

Stepping into the breezeway, I quietly pad down the concrete, the pitiful cry definitely belonging to a puppy. It gets louder the closer I get to the front of the building and as I turn the corner, there's a man squatted down behind the bushes.

My hand flies to my chest as I jump back.

All of a sudden, excruciating pain radiates through the back of my skull. A scream rips from my throat, but it fades into nothing as I'm plunged into darkness.

The first thing I notice when I wake up is my head throbbing like I'm being hit over and over.

Blinking my eyes open, I curse under my breath.

Fuck, even *that* hurts.

Reaching for my tender scalp, my fingers meet an angry knot, pulsing against my skull as I snatch my hand away.

Breathing deeply, I peel my eyes open, disoriented as I slowly gaze at the ceiling.

Where the fuck am I?

My chest feels heavy, my stomach churning as I remember being cracked on the head, passing out soon after. Staring blankly at the wood beams, coolness meets my hands as they settle on the floor.

Concrete.

I'm in a basement.

Summoning every bit of strength I have; I slowly push up on my elbows. The movement makes me dizzy, but I grit my teeth, pushing myself until I'm in a seated position, bracing against the rough texture of the wall.

The room is dark and cool, the faint smell of mildew and something I can't put my finger on hanging in the air. The walls are made of concrete blocks, crumbled pieces littering the floor. There's a small puddle in the corner, next to a rusted bucket. A chain is bolted to the wall, hanging loosely a few feet away.

Oh God.

I'm not the first captive to be held in this pit.

Swallowing the bile rising in my throat, I get to my knees, spotting a withered staircase behind me. It leads to a red door, a single yellow lightbulb lighting the steps.

My stomach clenches, dread sinking into my bones. I don't know who has taken me, but my mind circles back to the most likely suspect.

Colin.

He's found me.

I'm not sure how long I've been here, but the last memory of Dex seems so far away. He was running to the store to get more popcorn. He demanded I stay inside, and I agreed before he gave me his signature panty melting smile. He kissed me hard and left me breathless before leaving.

It was only when I heard a puppy crying a few minutes later, that I foolishly opened the front door. Slipping into the breezeway, I headed for the bushes, my heart constricting with every pitiful whimper the animal released.

I may not particularly like people, but I've always been a sucker for animals. The fluffier, the better. While reptiles are pretty, I've always refrained from touching them. It's weird petting something that doesn't have hair.

As the whimpers grew louder, I rounded the corner, coming face to face with some ass hat holding a rottweiler puppy in his arms, squeezing his body enough to make him cry out.

That's the last thing I remember before being knocked out.

Now I'm here, trapped in a basement by my uncle, I assume. It could be worse.

You could be chained to the wall.

Footsteps overhead draw my attention and I track them to the door. Reaching for my pocketknife, I'm pissed to realize I'm in my pajamas, so I don't have it.

Should have kept your ass inside like Dex told you to.

Scanning the room, I look for anything that could be used as a weapon, but I come up empty. My only option is to defend myself with the shit bucket in the corner.

I'm so fucked.

I don't know how the hell I'm going to get out of this.

I don't know how long I've been here.

Dex will never find me.

I'm alone once again.

My worst nightmare is now my reality.

The red door groans as it opens, an imposing figure making his way down the stairs. They sway slightly under his feet, and I silently hope he falls through them, being crushed by all the wood.

"She's awake at last." Colin's voice is a shock to my system.

I haven't heard it since the night he murdered my family.

I've lived in fear for two years.

I've tried so hard to prevent this from happening.

I've failed.

But instead of feeling the despair and numbness like before, something else rears its head.

My body tenses as I absorb the new emotions, letting them take over. It feels like a spiderweb being woven into place, a rightness I've never experienced settling over me.

A rebirth.

Fury.

A slow storm builds inside me, and I anchor myself to the eye, willing it to grow stronger.

Willing myself to embrace the chaos and focus on one thing.

Killing him.

"Savannah, you were always so beautiful. I'm glad you're here." Colin coos.

"You lured me outside with a puppy, you sick fuck."

"Ah. You always loved animals. It was easy to get your attention."

"What did you do with him?" I ask calmly, the undercurrent of my rage battling to break through the surface.

He shrugs. "I left him. He was the runt of the litter anyway."

I laugh bitterly. "You're such a piece of shit!"

"Your foul mouth surprises me, niece." He admonishes me and I flip him off.

"Yeah? Well, nothing about you surprises me, murderer."

"I'm sorry, Savannah. I wish I had killed you with your family to save you the pain of losing them."

My eyes widen a fraction. He's sorry for not killing me with them. Not for killing his own brother and his family. My pain obviously bothers him and if this wasn't such a fucked-up situation, I might laugh.

That night, my life went up in smoke and I lost everything.

My family.

My future.

My home.

And for what?

Fucking money.

My uncle wanted my dad to step away from the business. He would never do that. He wasn't a man who'd be content staying at home, piddling around and my uncle knew that.

"This useless chatter is boring me, *uncle.* If you're going to kill me, just do it."

"That was my original plan, but I have something else in store for you."

My blood runs cold.

Dex told me Colin added sex trafficking to his resume.

He chuckles darkly. "You're gorgeous, Savannah. You are worth more to me alive."

Something inside me snaps at his words. "I will fucking die before anyone touches me you sick motherfucker!"

He sighs. "Don't be so dramatic. One of my clients will buy you, have his fun and most likely kill you because of your mouth. I'm sure you won't suffer long."

Bile rises in my throat as I stand in front of my uncle, seeing another level of his depravity.

He grins smugly and I deflate for a moment. While I stand freely in this room without chains, I'm still trapped.

I have no weapons.

I have no back up.

I'm alone and defenseless.

My mind wanders to Dex and sadness fills my chest. I'd likely be cowered in the corner, crying hysterically with fear if it wasn't for him. He helped me tap into the old Savannah, a fighter. Not only did he guide me back to myself, but he also showed me how to build myself up, become stronger.

I'd give anything to feel his touch right now.

To hear him whisper strength against my ear.

To look into his eyes one last time and see what is hidden there, only for me.

My uncle wants to sell me to the highest bidder.

While that may be my fate, I won't take it lying down.

I'd rather die.

Fisting my hands at my sides, my resolve is clear as I remember I do have one weapon.

Myself.

"You're right. This will be quick."

His eyes widen as I brace my feet apart, posturing myself the way Dex showed me while we trained. My fists come up in front of me, ready to fight this motherfucker to the death.

He rolls his eyes. "Don't be ridiculous. I'd have to lower the price if I bruised the merchandise."

His words burn my skin like acid and a growl I've never heard rises from my chest. In an instant, I lunge forward, punching him in the throat. His hands fly up to circle his neck, choking on the little bits of air he's gasping for.

Seizing the moment, my right leg kicks out, his knee crunching as he hits the ground. He bellows brokenly in agony, and I reach for his side, snatching the knife from the sheath on his belt.

Raising the blade in the air, I smile. "How the tables have turned, *uncle.*"

Spitting the last word, a loud boom fills the air around me, the old house shaking to its foundation.

But it doesn't shake me.

I'm sturdy and strong, pissed off and determined.

Through the dirt and dust, I plunge the knife

into his chest, where his heart is supposed to be.

Chapter Nineteen

Declan

As soon as I step into the breezeway, I know something is wrong. The light from Savannah's apartment shines on the walkway and as I approach the door, my heart stops.

"Savannah!" I roar, running through the small apartment, searching for the other half of my soul. "Savannah!" She's not here and I'm losing my shit. "Savannah!"

Pulling out my phone, I open the tracking app. A blue dot pulses on my screen. It's showing her about thirty minutes away, but the dot isn't moving.

Does Colin have her?

Was he this close the entire time, slipping under the radar like the fucking snake he is?

Dialing Jase, my heart thunders while I wait for him to pick up.

"Yeah?"

"He fucking took her!" I scream, all of my control gone, *like my girl.*

"Send me the address. We're on our way." He demands, yelling for Rage.

"Bring the heavy shit with you." I bark, ending the call.

Jase always has my back. But in this moment, not even back up can soothe what's raging inside me.

My mind races with the possibility she may already be dead.

My stomach churns at the thought and I grit my teeth, refusing to accept it.

She's strong.

She's a fighter.

She won't give up.

After sending Jase the address, I pocket my phone heading for the door. I need to get to my apartment and gear up.

Turning the doorknob, a whimper stops me in my tracks. Jerking my head towards the sound, I spot a puppy cowering under the coffee table.

What the hell?

Savannah's door was open. I guess the little guy wandered inside.

Slowly reaching for him, I bring him to my chest. She told me one night she's always wanted a dog but put the idea on the back burner because of her lifestyle over the past two years.

"Hey, it's okay buddy." I whisper softly to the puppy. His ears perk up and he licks my chin, his paw coming up to rest on my jaw.

Once inside my unit, I put him on the floor, gathering guns and knives as he sniffs his new surroundings. With my vest on, I pack a weapon in every pocket and strap on the fucking thing.

As I reach the door, I turn towards the puppy. "Try not to fuck shit up too much. I'll bring you some food once I get your new momma back."

With that, I'm out the door, in my truck,

speeding through every stop sign and traffic light. The drive is a blur, my mind focused on one thing.

Getting my girl back.

"Two guards at the back of the house. Heard them talking about a girl in the basement." Jase tells me as soon as we meet up at the tree line a few hundred feet from the house.

He was closer to the old house than I was, so he texted me on my way, telling me where to pull off and meet them.

"I snuck up to the side of the house trying to see her through the windows. That's when I heard them talking. She's in the basement." Rage says, pulling a gun bag from her shoulder. "I brought the grenade launcher, too. Let's blast these motherfuckers and get our girl back."

Jase shakes his head and I grit my teeth, knowing I'm going to kill every bastard in that house for even looking at Savannah.

Rage elbows me in the side, pushing the grenade launcher into my hands. "Light 'em up, Dex."

I hesitate for a moment, worried the blast could crumble the house on top of her.

Rage squeezes my forearm. "She'll be fine. She's in a concrete room, underground. We just want to blast the guards."

We stalk from the woods as a unit, Rage with a pistol in hand, Jase with his AK-47. The two guards at the back of the house spot us and before they can alert anyone else, I aim the grenade launcher towards the garage, pulling the trigger.

It explodes instantly, fire surging in the air and smoke chasing the guards into the yard. As they run for their lives, I pull out my pistol, and the three of us kill every single person trying to flee.

Once all the bodies are lifeless on the grass, I take off running, storming through the house. I can barely see, but the flames from the fire lights up the basement door. It groans loudly as I swing it open, rushing down the steps into the darkened room.

Hitting the bottom step, I freeze as the dust settles, giving me a clear view of Savannah.

She's straddling Colin, yelling at his lifeless body, stabbing him in the chest.

Inching closer, I'm careful not to startle her.

She's spitting in his face.

Crying for the family she lost.

Taking her revenge on the man who took everything away from her.

She's covered in blood.

His chest looks like ground hamburger meat.

How many times has she stabbed him?

Glancing at her hand, the knife handle slipped down from where she lost her grip, digging into her palm. She probably doesn't feel it.

"Savannah." I say her name, but she doesn't hear me.

She's lost in a deadly haze.

Fuck.

She's the most gorgeous thing I've ever seen, bathed in blood, and filled with lethal retribution.

"Savannah." Squatting down beside her, I grab her wrist, before she digs the blade into her skin further.

She flinches at my touch, swinging her free hand towards my face. I grip her other wrist, her gaze finding mine. Her eyes are wild as she jerks out of my hold, standing from Colin's body on shaky legs.

She drops the knife to the ground, panting heavily, looking around the room as if she doesn't know where she is.

"Little chaos. It's me. I'm here to take you home." I reassure her, rising slowly.

She's like a feral animal, trapped and ready to fight her way out of the cage.

"It's me, little one. I'm here."

Our gazes lock.

My sweet girl looks wild and lost.

Slowly moving towards her, she takes a step back, shaking her head. Her chest heaves, her hands shaking uncontrollably.

She opens her mouth to say something, but nothing comes out.

I'm fucking helpless and it's killing me. Her mind is splintered at this moment, and I can't fix it for her. "Let it the fuck out, baby." I command.

Frozen to the spot, I'm cautiously waiting for her to pass out from the emotional overload. I've counted the steps to ensure I make it to her before she hits the ground.

Footsteps behind me catch my attention, but the clicking of a tongue lets me know its Jase and Rage.

Savannah doesn't see them. I'm not sure she sees me. Just as I'm about to say her name again, she moves.

She falls to her knees, throwing her head back to the ceiling, an agonizing scream tearing from her throat. My heart seizes in my chest, feeling her pain and fury release into the room, wrapping around us all. It's suffocating and unbearable, the pressure threatening to send me to my knees.

I've never seen another human being unleash something so raw, so terrifying.

Unable to take the distance any longer, I rush to her side, pulling her into my arms. She doesn't fight me, and as I crush her against me, the last of her voice dies.

Rising to my feet, I carry her outside, Jase and Rage following behind me. We make it back to our vehicles, no one speaking until we approach my truck.

"Cleanup is on their way. I'll check in tomorrow. Take care of her, Declan." Jase nods as his arm wraps around Rage's shoulders, steering her towards their truck.

Gently placing Savannah in the passenger seat, I close the door, jogging around to my side. Jumping inside, I steal a glance, and her eyes are closed. The drive is silent other than my brave girl's breathing.

Between the three of us, we took out fifteen guards tonight.

The only one that counts is the life that Savannah took.

Colin Banks is dead.

By her hand.

As much as I wanted to make the son-of-a-bitch suffer, I'm glad it was her. It may not feel like it now, but she needed this. Not in the scenario of being kidnapped and held captive, but things don't always play out the way we want.

All that matters now is he's dead.

Pulling into the apartment parking lot, I park the truck and carry her inside my unit. She stirs in my arms, and I want to put her to bed, but I don't want to wake up to an angry Savannah when she realizes she slept covered in Colin's blood all night.

"Dex." She whispers as we enter the bathroom.

"I'm here, baby. We need to get a shower and then you can sleep." Lowering her slowly, she braces against me as I remove our clothes.

Helping her into the shower, I follow behind her, wishing the damn thing was bigger.

Nudging her under the spray, we watch as the water runs red. Turning her around to face the wall, I grab the shampoo, massaging it into her scalp. She flinches as I work my fingers towards the bottom of her skull. I grit my teeth, feeling the huge knot there.

Fuck, I know it hurts. I'm careful as I rinse her

hair and grab my body wash, squirting some on a cloth. Scrubbing her body gently, I turn her back towards me so I can wash her front.

"You found me." She murmurs so low I almost don't hear it.

My chest caves. She sounds broken like when we first met, and I can't let her fall into that pit of emotions again. Meeting her eyes, I let her see the truth. "I'll always find you, Savannah."

With tears rimming her eyes, she whispers, "How?"

Glancing at her throat, my fingers graze the charm. "Your necklace has a tracker behind the stone."

Waiting for her anger or at least a shocked gasp, neither happens.

She steps into me, wrapping her arms around my waist, laying her head against my chest. "Thank you."

"Always, baby." I kiss the top of her head. "Go ahead and hop out. I'll be out in a few minutes."

She nods, placing a kiss over my heart. Stepping out of the shower, she grabs a towel, heading into the bedroom.

Scrubbing quickly, I rinse off and grab a towel. As I enter the bedroom, she's already snuggled in the bed, lying on her side, the blanket pulled up to her chin.

"I need to look at your hand."

"I don't need stitches. I wrapped it up." She murmurs.

I don't bother to dress before slipping in beside her. She didn't either. Pulling her close, I lean my forehead into hers, every part of our bodies touching all the way down to our toes.

"Are you okay?" I ask, breathing her air.

"I'm okay."

"Tell me the truth, little one." I demand, running the back of my fingers across her cheek.

"Two years of being terrified and angry. It all came to a head tonight. Two years of wanting him dead and to be the one who actually killed him. I lost it."

Kissing her gently, I whisper, "It's okay to let it out, baby. You were beautiful tonight. I'm so fucking proud of you."

She smiles. "I feel better now that it's over. Honestly, I'm just exhausted."

Tracing the seam of her lips with my thumb, I kiss her forehead. "Sleep, sweet girl."

"Night, Dex."

Her breathing shallows before I can reply, although I'm not sure she's ready to hear it.

I wake up to the bed shaking and open my eyes to see Savannah holding the puppy.

Fuck!

I forgot about him. He's probably starving.

The bright smile on her face rivals the sun and I know my life would be over without her.

I don't seem to exist as she makes kissy noises at the puppy, letting him paw and lick her face. She giggles like a little girl and the sound erases every dark spec from my soul.

"I'm assuming we have a dog now?" I grin as she looks at me with twinkling eyes.

"Can we keep him, please?" She begs.

Reaching over to pet the little shit that is stealing my girl's attention, I nod. "He's yours, baby."

She bounces on the mattress, holding the puppy in the air. "I knew you were special when I saw you last night."

My body tenses. "What do you mean, when you saw him last night?"

She answers absentmindedly, never looking away from her new best friend. "After you left to get popcorn, I heard a puppy whining. It was so loud. I went outside to see if it was hurt. A guy was in the bushes, squeezing him to make him cry. That's when someone hit me in the back of the head and kidnapped me."

My mouth drops open. I was going to question her about how she was taken, but I wanted her to rest first. "Put the puppy down."

She frowns but sits him on the bed, where he runs to the end, chewing on the corner of the blanket.

I grip her wrist, pulling her on top of me. Crushing her to my body, cradling her head against my chest, my mind finally processes how close I was to losing her. How close I was to losing everything.

Her head rises from my chest. "I think I'm in love with you." She bites her bottom lip, looking everywhere but at me.

My eyes drift closed, inhaling the sweet scent of her vulnerability. This is all I've wanted since the moment I first saw her. "I *know* you're in love with me."

She purses her lips, finally meeting my gaze. "How do you *know*?"

"Because I love you with every fucking breath in my body. My heart beats for you. My soul searches for you when you're not here. You were created for me as I was for you. That's how I *know*."

"Dex." She whispers, her bottom lip quivering.

"I love you beyond the ends of the earth. Beyond anything the human mind can fathom. I will protect you until the end of time. I will rip apart your enemies and bring you their hearts."

She swallows slowly, a lone tear leaking from the corner of her eye.

Leaning forward, my tongue darts out, tasting the salty emotion before it drips from her jawline. "You're mine, little chaos and there's nothing you can do about it."

She grins. "Prove it."

Flipping her onto her back, I hold her gaze. "You're such a fucking brat." I growl, trailing my tongue down her body, needing to taste her.

She grips my hair, stopping me. "Later. I need your cock, now."

My grin is feral as her pupils blow wide. Rising

to my knees, my hands skim her inner thighs until I reach her soaked cunt. Spreading her swollen lips, I hold them open as I slide inside her just a few inches. She moans my name and I'm lost to the little noises coming from her lips. Her pink pussy swallows me with every thrust and I'm hypnotized by the sight.

Needing to hear her beg, my strokes become shallow, my slow pace maddening even to me.

"Dex, please!" She pleads.

Plunging deep, we both groan, clinging onto each other, like the other may disappear.

"I fucking love you, little chaos. Until my last breath, I'll always love you." I growl against her ear, my cock driving into her pussy like my life depends on it.

"I love you, Dex." She moans and the sound has me slamming inside her over and over, my piercings hitting her g-spot just the way she likes it.

She nudges my chest, and I pull away as she rises from the mattress, pushing me onto my back. She straddles me quickly, taking my cock inside her. "I don't know what to do, but I want to ride you."

My eyes roll back in my head as her curvy hips roll back and forth perfectly. "Just like that, baby. Fuck, just like that."

"You like?" She asks, grinning mischievously.

She lifts her hips, slamming down hard, and my balls tighten. "You're going to make me come if you keep that up."

My hands slide up her torso, cupping her perky tits. Squeezing them roughly, she whimpers. Pinching her nipples, she grinds her hips, and I feel her pussy clench around me. Dropping my hand between her thighs, I flick her clit, and she loses control.

"Don't stop, Dex!" She whines and my cock throbs painfully, ready to pump her full of cum.

"Come." I demand and she obeys, screaming my name as her body convulses above me.

Her pussy strangles my cock, literally sucking my cum and my soul from my body.

We grind against each other, drawing out our orgasms until she collapses on my chest.

"Not bad for a newbie, huh?" She pants.

My girl needs reassurance and I'm too fucking happy to give it to her. Wrapping my arms around her waist, I kiss the top of her head. "If you don't ride me every morning, I'll throw a fucking man-tantrum."

She giggles, her warm breath fanning across my chest.

I smile, but it's short lived as small, needle pointed teeth latch onto my big toe. "Ouch, you little fucker."

Savannah shoots up, laughing as she scoops up the little troublemaker, sitting him between us.

"I meant to get him food last night, but I forgot. We need to go to the pet store and get him what he needs." I say, trying to pet the little bad ass, but he keeps biting my fingers.

"I took him out before you woke up. Surprisingly, he didn't have any accidents. I gave him some sandwich meat until we could get him some food and put a bowl of water on the floor. Colin bred them and didn't care about this one because he's the runt."

She frowns, and I know there must've been a conversation between them last night about using the puppy to get her out of the apartment.

Sick fuck.

"He needs a name."

Her eyes light up. "Can I name him?"

"Sure, baby."

She watches him for a while, and I know the moment she settles on a name.

"His name is Storm."

Chapter Twenty

Savannah

It's been a week since I killed Colin.

The most peaceful week I've had in over two years.

Storm has settled in well, especially since Dex bought half the toys and treats in the store, and a dog bed that's bigger than the couch in my apartment. He may call him a little fucker, but the sexy hitman has a soft spot for our ferocious puppy.

We've been staying at his place every night, and I don't mind. I like being in his space. He's constantly sending me links to houses in different cities, patiently waiting for me to make up my mind.

Our relationship has been a whirlwind. While it's overwhelming to plan a future with him so quickly, nothing has ever felt so right.

We fit together perfectly.

He understands my chaotic mind.

He encourages my darkness to come out and play.

While he's my protector, he's shown me I can protect myself.

As I slip into bed, Dex has already dozed off after a long day of research on a new mark. He stirs, turning onto his side, pulling me into his chest. Breathing in his masculine scent, my eyes drift closed as I soak in his warmth and fall asleep.

Something startles me awake.

My eyes dart around the bedroom, engulfed in darkness except for the sliver of light shining through the curtains from the streetlight outside.

Tilting my head, I listen for whatever woke me up, but I don't hear anything. Glancing at Dex, he's sound asleep.

Maybe it was a dream.

My eyes barely close before I hear a loud bang on the front door, and I bolt upright like I've been struck by lightning.

Sliding out of bed quietly, I creep around the side, grabbing Dex's gun from his nightstand. Thankfully, Storm is passed out on his new bed, his little alligator plush toy tucked under one leg.

Grabbing my t-shirt from the floor, I slip it over my head. Tip-toeing from the bedroom, I silently make my way through the apartment, racking the slide, a bullet in the chamber.

I don't know who the fuck is beating on the door, but they're about to have a bad night.

As I approach the front door, I look through the peephole, but I don't see anyone. I press my ear against the cool wood, listening for any sign of someone outside.

I should've woken up Dex.

It's a fleeting thought I push away because I've got this. I've killed people. I can handle some jackass beating on a door.

Another loud bang sounds, the force of it rattling the door against my face. Swallowing a surprised yelp, I look through the peephole again. Before my eyes have time to focus, the door bursts open.

I'm pushed back from the impact, but luckily the wall stops my momentum before I hit the floor. Catching my breath, I look up to see who I'm about to empty my clip into.

A fucking giant wearing a sinister grin steps through the threshold, a crowbar in his hand.

Pushing myself away from the wall, I angle my back towards the hall. Lifting my gun into the air, I point it at his chest. "Who the fuck are you?"

"I came to collect the boss's merchandise." He smirks, taking a step towards me.

Retreating a step, my index finger twitches on the trigger. "Sorry dick face, I'm not for sale."

"Stupid girl. Did you think your uncle was the end?" His expression morphs into murder and it's fucking terrifying. "Boss will be pissed if I leave visible marks on you, but it might just be worth it." He moves closer.

"If you take one more step, I'll empty this entire clip in your chest, you big motherfucker."

"Come on, bitch, let's play." He grins and my killer switch flips.

Game on.

Storm comes running from the bedroom, barking, and raising hell like he's about to eat the asshole trying to kidnap me. Just as Storm reaches him, he kicks his foot out and I snap, pulling the trigger before he can strike my puppy.

With how good a shot I am, I'm disappointed when the bullet lodges in his shoulder. He stumbles back a few steps, only to regain his composure.

Storm runs to my side, and I bend down, scooping him into my arms.

Fuck!

If he gets his hands on me, I'm dead.

Spinning on my heel, I take off running towards the bedroom, knowing there's a shotgun behind the door. As I reach the edge of the room, a hand darts out, pulling me through the doorway. I stumble, hitting the floor hard. Storm yelps even though he's not hurt, and he runs into the bathroom to hide.

Stay there, my little protector.

My head whips around just as Dex steps into the hallway, firing three shots simultaneously, a loud thud signaling the big son-of-a-bitch has fallen. Gurgling sounds follow and I can't believe he isn't dead yet.

He has to be some kind of asylum experiment.

Dex disappears from my line of sight, and I crawl across the floor until I reach the threshold of the room. Looking to my right, my breath catches as I watch him stand over the intruder, bashing him in the face with the butt of the shotgun. My body flinches with every strike, the man's face resembling raw hamburger meat.

Dex is brutal when he loses his shit, and I can't look away. He's fucking beautiful and hypnotic, trapping me in his violent little bubble. I could watch him unleash his wrath all day, falling more in love with every deadly blow he delivers.

He turns suddenly, dropping the shotgun, his chest heaving. His lethal expression is unnerving, as I've never seen him like this before. He strides towards me, reaching down, pulling me to my feet. "Are you okay?"

"Y-yeah." I whisper, focused on his black eyes, wondering if the devil has rented out his body for a little while.

He looks like a rabid animal, covered in blood, ready to attack anyone who dares to come close.

His hand rises to my face, his thumb trailing across my bottom lip, tugging it down as he bites his own.

He glides his rough fingers down my throat and the front of my thin shirt. Watching his hand travel down my body, I take in the trail of blood he's leaving behind.

Marking me.

Claiming me.

He leans in, his warm breath caressing my ear. "No one will ever hurt you again. I'll kill every motherfucker who dares to even look at you."

A pathetic sound escapes my lips as he traces the shell of my ear with his warm tongue. His blood-soaked hand slides between my thighs, his fingers gliding easily through my arousal.

He growls, walking me backwards into the bedroom, the anticipation making my body tremble. "Be a good girl and bend over the bed."

My body submits willingly, turned on by blood, murder, and the crazed look in Dex's eyes.

The back of my knees hit the mattress and I spin around, bending over for him. My body jolts as he slaps my ass, a deep moan rising from my chest. He smacks me again, the sting of his palm bringing me closer to the edge.

He steps closer, kicking my legs apart with his foot. Gripping my hip, he slides his hard cock through my slickness, easing the tip inside me.

There's no preparation, no foreplay.

Dex is starving and so am I.

He slams into me, stretching my pussy beyond its limit, but I still want more. Moaning his name, I push back against him, begging for his brutal rhythm.

His chest presses against my back, his weight pushing me deeper into the mattress. His arm sneaks underneath me, his fingers demanding entry inside my mouth.

"Suck." He commands, pressing two fingers between my lips.

Sucking his fingers like my life depends on it, he groans, thrusting inside me faster and harder.

"Fuck, Dex." I sob around his fingers, my body oversensitive with the need to come.

"Your tight cunt will be the death of me." He growls as the bed shakes, our sweat slicked skin sliding against each other in the most erotic way.

The familiar pull in my lower belly rises, my breathing coming in short pants. I can't form a single thought, or word as he fucks me within an inch of my life.

He pulls his fingers from my mouth, wrapping his hand around my throat. "Come for me. Soak my cock with your cum."

The dam breaks, an obscene amount of liquid squirting from my pussy. I scream his name, my body convulsing as I cry out with every stroke of his cock, dragging out my pleasure. Everything disappears and there is no sense of time. I'm trapped in a cloud of euphoria, surrounded by death and Dex. The combination is everything I need and through the fog, my love for this man intensifies, knowing I will kill for him as he does for me.

I will do anything to protect him.

To protect us.

"Fuck!" He roars, filling me to the hilt, emptying himself inside me as his piercings rub soothingly against my inner walls.

I'm pinned beneath him, his cock twitching inside me as I struggle to catch my breath from an earth-shattering orgasm.

After a few moments, he rises to his feet, bringing me with him. Wrapping an arm around my waist, he secures me against him, knowing I can't support myself on sex drunk legs.

Leaning down, he kisses my neck. "You

squirted, baby. I'm hard again just thinking about it."

Huffing out a laugh, I turn in his arms, slowly. "I need a little recovery time after that, big guy."

He smirks, bringing his lips to mine. "Was it too much, little one?"

Shaking my head, I grin. "Hell no."

He exhales deeply, kissing my forehead. "I need to call for a cleanup."

"Maybe a little extra help this time. Moving gigantor in there won't be easy."

He chuckles. "True."

"You were sleeping like the dead."

His face turns serious. "The door busted open, and it woke me up. I don't usually sleep that hard. I'm sorry, baby."

"It's okay. Today was a long day." I kiss him gently. "How did he know it was us?"

"I'm assuming your uncle contacted him. Probably to let him know he secured you."

"He was going to sell me." My teeth clench and I'm pissed all over again.

"He *thought* he was going to sell you. No one will touch you, but me. I'll always protect you. Do you understand?"

Sighing heavily, I nod. "I know."

"We're going to stay at your place since I don't have a fucking door anymore. Grab the puppy and let's go."

"Yes, sir." I retort and his eyes darken again.

Oh shit...

Chapter Twenty-One

Declan

"He's a bad ass!" I yell through the apartment.

Savannah stomps into the bedroom, her hands flying to her hips. "He's a baby!"

"He's a fucking menace." I grumble, staring at the white fuzzy shit all over the floor.

As if he was summoned, the chubby asshole comes trotting in the room like he owns the damn place.

"Dex, you need to chill. He's teething." She kneels down, rubbing his ears, talking to him like a baby.

He cuts his eyes at me, and I swear the little fucker grins.

Creepy bastard.

My irritation disappears as I watch her face light up.

Storm isn't so bad.

He's almost adorable when he's asleep, but destructive as hell when he's awake.

In the two weeks we've had him, he's destroyed three beds and countless toys. He chewed up my favorite boots and Savannah's flip flops. She hasn't lost her patience with him, those puppy dog eyes and round belly earning him a pass for every bad deed.

I have to admit, I've never been more content than when we watch movies at night with two bowls of popcorn because she insists on sharing with him.

My life is complete, Savannah and even Storm, filling every empty part of me.

I've waited my entire life to feel this.

Love.

I wasn't sure I was able to feel the emotion, but Savannah changed that.

Even more, I never thought anyone would love me, but she changed that, too.

Her love has chased away my demons, self-loathing, and abandonment issues, now nowhere to be found. We've formed an unbreakable bond and I'll burn this fucking world to keep her by my side and in my arms. I'll kill anyone who tries to harm her. I'll give my life to protect her.

And I'll give her all the badass puppies she wants to see her smile the way she is now.

She rises to her feet, her hips swaying as she saunters over to me, wearing a mischievous grin.

Reaching out, I pull her into my arms, and she squeals as I crush her to me. Her arms wrap around my waist as she buries her face in my chest.

Sighing heavily, I kiss the top of her head. "Get his leash. Let's go get him another bed to eat."

She lifts her head, gazing at me with that look that tells me everything I need to know.

She loves me.

"I love you too, little chaos."

Storm barks and as we look his way, he's rolling around on his back, white fuzz sticking to his fur.

He better be glad he's cute...

"Should we wait until he's out of his destructive phase before we move?" Savannah asks on our way home from the pet store.

"It'll be fine, baby."

"So, you really did like the house we looked at yesterday?"

"I did, but I want you to pick a house you love. My home is wherever you are." I glance in her direction and her eyes are glassy with unshed tears. I grip her hand. "It's you and me, little one. And the little demon in the back seat."

She giggles and I'll never get tired of hearing that sound.

My phone rings and I nod for her to grab it from my pocket.

"It's Jase." She tells me.

"Put it on speaker." She presses the button, holding it towards me. "Yeah?"

"Is Savannah with you?" He asks.

"She's right here. Why?"

"I've got information on the guy who broke into your apartment. He works for a man named Richard Long. He's a key player in the trafficking world. Colin worked for him, and he owns the safehouse where Colin took Savannah."

Pulling into the apartment's lot, I park and turn the truck off, but neither of us move.

Jase continues. "Colin contacted him as soon as he kidnapped Savannah, and they struck a deal for her."

My vision clouds as rage takes over. I suspected this, but hearing it confirmed has me white knuckling the steering wheel, fighting my demons for control.

Her small hand grips my thigh, and we lock eyes as she shifts closer. Wrapping my arm around her shoulders, I pull her into my side. "What's the plan, Hamilton?"

"Chances are, he'll send others to take her, Dex."

My heart thunders in my chest. "We found a house about an hour from here. We'll go ahead and move."

"What if he already has someone watching us?" Savannah asks and my fists clench at the worry in her eyes.

In a world full of options, there's only one for me.

Her.

I'll kill every motherfucker who gets in the way of our future. She's my life, my heart, my soul.

No one will take her from me.

Jase interrupts my spiraling thoughts. "Rage has an idea."

"Let's hear it." I demand.

"She wants to draw them out."

Silence.

I feel Savannah's stare, but I don't spare her a glance before taking the phone from her hand. "Absolutely fucking not."

"Dex-" He starts.

"No! Would you use Rage as bait? Have you lost your fucking mind?" Jumping out of the truck, I'm shaking, trying not to lose my shit. Holding the phone to my ear with my shoulder, I open the passenger door, gripping her hand.

She holds Storm in her free arm, carrying him like a toddler on her hip.

Little moments like this are why I love her so much.

Of course, its ruined by the asshole on the other end of the line. "It's not like that. Hear me out. We aren't going to leave her alone. She'll be with Rage, and we'll be close by."

We go inside her apartment and sit on the couch. She holds the puppy, petting him continuously as I watch her. The gears are turning in her mind, and I'm terrified she'll want to go along with this bullshit.

He goes on to tell me his grand fucking plan, which I hate but we listen anyway. Once he's finished, I end the call abruptly.

"I like the plan." Savannah says confidently.

"You expect me to be okay with this?" I ask incredulously.

"You don't have to like it." She grips my hand. "I want this to be over. I want us to start our life together without all the shit hanging over us."

"Savannah-"

She cuts me off. "I want to do this. Please, Dex. Please help me end this."

My heart stops, seeing the desperation in her eyes. She's never asked me for a damn thing other than Storm. She doesn't like asking for help, but she's asking me now.

Everything in my head is screaming to tell her no.

Knowing the risk is too high.

One wrong move and I could lose her.

But if I deny her this, deny her our future, I'll definitely lose her.

My love for her wins and I know this is our only option.

I'll be there to protect her. I'll keep her safe.

Leaning over, I pick up the puppy, putting him on the floor. Gripping her by the waist, I pull her onto my lap, and she straddles me.

She watches me cautiously, and I hate the look in her eyes.

Wrapping my hand around her throat, I pull her closer. "I'll never deny you anything, little chaos."

She smiles. "I'll never take advantage of that."

"I know, baby."

Chapter Twenty-Two

Savannah

Our plan is solid.

Dex doesn't like it, but he knows deep down this is the only way I can be free.

Did I expect everything to come together this fast? *No.*

Did it? *Yes.*

Jase conveniently leaked our new address so it would get back to Richard Long. Everything else fell into place. Now, we sit and wait.

While Dex and I plan on buying a house, we decided on a little rental until we sort out this mess. We left those shitty apartments behind and put most of our belongings in storage. We figured there's no point in bringing it all here when this place will soon be a memory too.

We have men watching the house, guys that everyone trusts from the organization. They're well hidden, while the four of us have sat in this house for days like sitting ducks.

And this house is *small.*

Two bedrooms and one bathroom being shared between four people and a growing rottweiler.

It's been rough.

I'm grateful to have them all here, willing to protect me and help me through this, but sharing a bathroom with three other people is too much.

And Rage eats all my damn popcorn.

A small price to pay, *I guess.*

The back door opens and Storm barrels through the house, Dex and Jase not far behind. This place has a fence in the yard, so he loves being able to run and play off his leash. He's reached his awkward puppy phase where his body is lanky, and his legs are long. He trips over everything, but it doesn't slow him down.

Storm and Dex are my life now.

Dex is everything I never knew I needed.

Storm is the not so little bundle of joy I've always wanted.

Once this shit show blows over, my life will be perfect with my boys.

I'm woken up by Dex shaking me, Rage and Jase standing in the bedroom doorway, pistols drawn.

I try to speak, but he puts his finger to my lips and whispers, "They're here. The house is surrounded."

My chest tightens, knowing this is it.

We'll either take out the threat or die trying.

It's strange.

For two years, I wanted to die. It consumed my thoughts day in, day out.

Now, I'm railing against death, willing to do anything in my power to stay alive.

Not only for Dex and Storm, but for myself.

For my family.

I want to live, and these motherfuckers are

about to see just how much.

Slipping out of bed, I slide on my jeans and shoes, grabbing my nine-millimeter off the nightstand. Opening the drawer, I reach for my knife, sliding it in my back pocket. "I'm ready."

He nods to Jase and Rage, and they disappear. Pulling me into his arms, he crushes me to his chest. "You can do this, Savannah. I'll be right there with you."

"I love you, Archer." I whisper, holding onto him like it's the last time.

It may be.

"I love you, Banks." He crashes his lips to mine, a soul crushing kiss stealing my breath.

He pulls away, tracing every inch of my face like he's burning it into his memory. Seeing him look at me this way is too much.

He meets my gaze, his eyes darkening with madness that only the devil could rival. "Kill them all."

I grin. "Every last motherfucker."

He grips my hand, pulling me towards the door, but I stop him. "Where's Storm?"

"Rage locked him in the bathroom."

Without another word, we leave the room, creeping through the quiet house hand in hand. Dex has me tucked behind him, ready to shield me from whatever is waiting for us.

Glass breaks in the living room and as we turn the corner, Rage's manic laugh makes the hair on my neck stand up. "Just in time, boys! I was getting bored waiting on you."

Two men climb through the window at the same time the front door bursts open. Three more guys barrel into the house and I raise my gun.

Bullets fly across the room, spraying the walls and furniture. I pull the trigger, shooting one asshole in the neck. He clutches his throat, falling to the floor, his desperate gurgles being drowned out by the chaos around us.

Rage has a guy pinned to the ground, stabbing him in the chest. Jase shoots two guys simultaneously between their eyes. Dex is fighting one of them, beating the living shit out of him.

This is all out fucking war and we're holding our own on the battlefield.

Movement at the door catches my eye as a man in a suit walks in, flanked by two men, four more behind him.

Rage huffs as she stands up, Jase turning to face our guests. A crack sounds next to me as Dex snaps his victim's neck, his head bouncing off the floor as he releases him. He jumps to his feet, trying to shield me from the men.

The one in the suit raises his hands. "I'm sorry for the intrusion. I told them to knock." He smirks, his eyes boring into mine.

"Who the fuck are you?" Dex demands, pushing me behind him.

"My name is Richard Long. I believe you know who I am Mr. Archer." He grins, never taking his eyes off me. "I believe you also know that Miss

Banks belongs to me, courtesy of her uncle."

My breathing slows as I focus on his words. Everything that's happened over the past two years has led to this moment.

My family's murders.

My isolation.

Killing my uncle.

Now, Richard Long.

He's the last obstacle, the only thing standing between me and my future with Dex.

This ends now.

Dex reaches behind him, gripping my shirt to pull me closer. Staring down Richard, he growls. "If you touch one fucking hair on her head, I will rip your fucking heart out and feed it to our dog."

Dex let's go of my shirt, his fingers moving in a sequence, like he's giving a signal for something.

From the corner of my eye, I see Jase moving towards me slowly. Rage is behind him, protected by her big ass hitman.

Long chuckles. "Savannah will be coming-"

Dex cuts him off, raising his gun. "Don't say her name, motherfucker."

"Go ahead, Declan. Shoot me. The six men surrounding me will kill you all on the spot, including *Savannah*." He mockingly says my name again and Dex snaps.

He lunges forward, tackling Long to the ground. Raising my gun, I rapidly fire at the two guys closest to Dex. Jase does the same taking out two more with his signature head shots.

Rage abandons her knife, shooting another one in the chest.

There's one left, but the back door crashes open and Rage and I whirl around to find another hoard of men stalking in, guns raised.

Fuck!

My body whirls as two shots ring out behind us, Dex blowing Richard's brains all over the floor, then shooting the sixth man in the chest.

He springs forward, but before he makes it to me, the click of a hammer being pulled back catches my attention.

Everything happens in the blink of an eye.

I have a split second to make a choice.

No one else I care about will die.

The guy aims his gun at Rage.

Jase can't live without her. I've witnessed the love between them and it's the all-consuming, once in a lifetime connection we all dream of. The most beautiful thing I've ever seen.

Okay, the *second* most beautiful thing.

My love for Dex is so deeply woven into who I am, it brought me back to life.

It gave me purpose.

It gave me hope.

I want the love he willingly gives me every single day.

I want a life with him.

I want to be happy.

But I have to choose.

Please forgive me, Dex.

The thought of losing him or anyone else I care about ignites my blood with fury and I burst into action.

Jase reaches for her, his own gun firing, followed by Dex emptying his magazine at the rest of the men. The man Dex shot in the chest earlier is still alive somehow and he raises a knife, stabbing Jase in the back of the leg.

He falls to the floor, roaring Rage's name.

Rage screams as the shot is fired, her focus on Jase instead of the bullet coming her way.

Time slows to a crawl, Dex's screams fading in the distance.

My feet move on their own, tackling Rage to the floor. We hit the ground hard as the bullet enters my side. She reaches for her thigh, unsheathing a throwing star before flipping us where she's covering my body, launching it through the air. Turning my head, I watch the death star fly, hitting the guy in the jugular before he crumples to the ground.

Jase groans as he stands, pulling the knife from his calf muscle. He grabs his gun from the floor just as Dex's murderous roar fills the room.

Rage's head snaps up. "Oh shit!"

"Help him, please. Kill them all." I croak, the pain in my side making me nauseous.

A sinister smile forms on her lips. "I'm staying with you, Chaos. Our men are fucking devils, they don't need me."

I wince as she applies pressure to my wound.

I can't bring myself to look at it, any movement making me cringe.

Finding Dex with my gaze, he's bloody and beautiful, fighting beside Jase. He's opted to holster his gun, using a machete to slice through the last of the men.

Where did he get a fucking machete?

I want one.

Especially when I see the guy's arm slide across the floor.

Taking in my crazy new friend, I see the pride on her face as she watches Jase and Dex kill every last one of the assholes. Her genuine smile makes me want to laugh.

She's a crazy bitch, but I like her.

She catches my eye, and her face softens. "I don't know what you were thinking taking a bullet for me but thank you. Dex is going to kick your ass and I'm going to laugh, but you have my gratitude."

Yep. She's crazy.

"I couldn't let Jase lose you." I whisper.

Her eyes shimmer with unshed tears. "Your heart is too fucking big, Savannah." She wipes her eyes with her free hand, keeping pressure on my wound with the other. "Lucky for you, I'm not going to let you die today."

The house is silent all of a sudden and Dex enters my line of sight as he drops the machete. Rage moves back, letting him inspect my side. A growl leaves his chest, and he looks up at Jase. "We have to go now!"

He scoops me into his arms, the pain dulling as the cold seeps into my bones. My eyes flutter, and he presses harder against my wound. "Savannah, stay awake for me, baby."

"It's okay, Dex." I murmur and I don't believe my own lie.

We only just found each other and now I'm going to die.

For two years, I wished for death. I couldn't bring myself to take my own life. Something always held me back.

Now, I know what it was.

Who it was.

Fate knew Dex would find me and I needed to hold on until he did.

"I love you, Declan." I whisper, trembling in his arms.

He clenches his jaw. "I won't let you die, Savannah."

It's not his choice if I leave this world today, but I smile the best I can through the pain, lifting my weak hand to his face. "I know."

We make it to Jase's truck, and he gently lays me in the back seat. Jase and Rage climb in the front as Dex moves in beside me. He places my head in his lap, running his fingers through my hair as the truck speeds off. His other hand keeps pressure on my wound, and I barely feel it anymore.

Opening my eyes, my heart shatters into

infinite pieces. He's worried and lost, a lone tear sliding down his cheek. It lingers on his jawline for a moment before falling to my chest, and I sigh, knowing a part of him will stay with me.

My body feels weak as I lose more blood. "I couldn't let anyone else die." I murmur as my eyes droop.

Understanding fills his eyes, but his jaw clenches. "I won't lose you." He chokes on his emotions, the tears flowing freely now. "I'm nothing without you. If you go, I go with you."

"Dex." I breathe, his name the last word I speak.

"No, Savannah. You can't give up. I love you and I won't live in a world where you don't exist."

He lifts his head, meeting Rage's gaze. She looks between us, reaching for Jase's hand. "Hurry, baby."

I'm barely lucid as the truck whips into the emergency room parking lot.

"We'll go get help." Rage says, running to Jase's door to help him out, leaving Dex and I alone.

"After you've recovered, I'm going to spank your ass, little one." He opens the door, cradling me in his arms. He sprints towards the entrance as the nurses meet us with a gurney. He gently lays me down, holding my hand as they rush me inside the building.

As the fog closes in, I finally rest my eyes. It's almost a peaceful feeling and I brace myself as it consumes me.

I'm on the verge of letting go when I hear, "Don't fucking leave me, Savannah!" He sounds far away, but the panic in his voice makes me want to fight.

Fight for myself.

Fight for us.

For our future.

I *will* come back to him.

Jase needs Rage.

Declan needs me.

It's a realization that makes me fight with everything I have, but I lose the battle as I'm plunged into darkness, Dex's voice fading to nothing.

Chapter Twenty-Three

Declan

I've never been this scared in my fucking life.

Savannah is in surgery, and we've been sitting in this waiting room with no word for what seems like hours.

I've paced back and forth so much; Rage told me I'm wearing a hole in the floor. She's trying to lighten the mood, but it can't be done.

Not until I know she's okay.

I can't lose her.

Without her, there is no me.

If she doesn't pull through, they'll have to put me in the ground with her.

Jase and Rage came in to wait with me after his leg got stitched up. It's a deeper wound, but he'll heal without any nerve damage. He hasn't complained once.

None of us have.

We're all beat to hell and back from the showdown at the house, but nothing else matters except Savannah.

We underestimated Richard Long. He brought a small army with him, and we didn't expect it. We knew he was a bigger player than Colin, but we didn't realize how badly he wanted her. Colin must've sold her at a steep price.

Fuck, I think I'm going to be sick.

Glancing at the clock on the wall, it's been two

hours since I've heard a word about her.

"Sit down big guy." Rage says gently.

"I can't. If I don't move, I'm going to lose my shit."

"Let him be, baby." Jase murmurs to Rage and her eyes soften, remembering when they were shot and the PTSD she suffered afterwards.

"The cops bought our story about the home invasion." Rage says in a hopeful voice.

Jase nods. "They know Richard Long, but they don't know us. They think we were unsuspecting victims."

"How do we explain the dismembered guys?" She asks with a grin.

"We have a couple of guys on the force. They'll take care of it." Jase shrugs.

Glancing down the hallway for the millionth time, the doctor who wheeled Savannah into surgery is walking towards me. Meeting him halfway, I grip his bicep. "Is she okay?"

He nods slowly. "She's stable. The bullet missed her right kidney, pancreas, and liver. It was lodged in the muscle, but we were able to remove it and stitch her up."

Falling to my knees, I sob into my hands, finally able to breathe for the first time in hours.

The doctor squeezes my shoulder. "Collect yourself son while we move her to a room. A nurse will come get you." His footsteps fade as I silently thank whoever is listening for saving her life.

And mine.

Hands grip my biceps, pulling me to my feet. Opening my eyes, Rage is on one side, Jase on the other.

She wipes my tears away, smiling sweetly. "Chaos thinks you're such a bad ass, Dex. Don't ruin it now."

"Jesus." Jase mutters and I huff out a laugh.

The nurse comes, and I follow her down the hall, the other two members of my family by my side.

She holds the door open and the three of us file into the room, the air knocked out of me as I see Savannah hooked up to multiple machines and an IV.

"Hey. It's okay, Dex. She's okay. They're just watching her vitals and making sure she stays hydrated. It was the same with me." Rage whispers, squeezing my hand for support.

Reaching for the chair against the wall, I slide it to the side of her hospital bed, taking her hand in mine. Her skin is pale and cool to the touch. Even though she's okay, my stomach twists and my chest constricts seeing her like this.

Jase walks to the other side of the bed, gritting his teeth, trying to mask his pain. More for Rage's benefit than his own. He carefully squeezes Savannah's hand. "We'll see you when you wake up, brave girl."

Stepping back, Rage takes his place. She cups her cheek, whispering something into her ear that we can't hear. It's strange seeing her like this, but

Savannah saved her life, so I know she's feeling emotional. She looks at me and smiles. "We'll give you some time alone. Call us when she wakes up. I'm going to take my husband home. As much as he's pretending to be alright, I see through that shit."

Jase rolls his eyes and I grin. "I'll check in later boss man. Take it easy."

The door closes behind them and I watch Savannah breathe, the beeping from the machines fading away. I'm in a daze, silently watching her chest rise and fall in rhythm with mine.

She's breathing.

She's still with me.

She's okay.

The exhaustion settles in, and I lay my head on the side of the bed next to her hip. Holding her hand, I drift off to sleep knowing she'll still be here when I wake up.

Tiny fingers glide through my hair, and I'd recognize that touch anywhere. Coming to slowly, I grin, until everything crashes down and my eyes snap open.

My head jerks up, my eyes colliding with the bright green ones I thought I'd never see again.

She smiles weakly. "Hi." Her voice is hoarse, and I jump up, pouring her a glass of water.

"Hey baby." Holding the glass, I aim the straw towards her mouth.

She sips the water slowly and once she's

finished, I set it on the side table, sitting on the edge of the hospital bed.

"How do you feel?" I ask, stroking her cheek with my thumb.

She leans into my touch, closing her eyes. "It hurts, but I'm glad to be alive."

I've never heard sweeter words leave her mouth except for when she told me she loved me. They break me apart and put me back together in the span of two seconds.

She wants to live.

She wants to be here.

With me.

Emotion clogs my throat as I speak. "Fuck, Savannah. I thought I lost you again."

She grips my hand, lacing our fingers together. "Don't you know, Archer? I'm yours. You'll never lose me."

Tears well in her eyes, matching my own and I lean down carefully, kissing her softly. "And I'm yours, little chaos. For eternity."

She caresses my cheek with her cool fingers. "Is Jase okay?"

I nod. "He's okay. No damage and they stitched him up."

She sighs in relief. "And Rage?"

"She's alive because of you." I tell her.

"Are you mad at me?" She asks nervously.

"Yes."

She deflates.

While I'm furious she put herself in the line

of fire, I'm so fucking proud of her for being the fearless woman I knew she was.

Taking pity, I put her at ease. "Don't worry, little chaos. I'll forgive you once you're my wife."

Her jaw drops, her eyes widening. "Wait. What?"

"We're getting married when you're released from the hospital." I smirk, daring her to object.

"You're not going to ask me?"

"No."

"Why not?"

"Are you mine?"

She nods.

"Am I yours?"

She nods again.

"Then there's no need to ask."

She shakes her head, a faint smile tugging at her lips. "Smug bastard."

"I sure am. I stole the heart of the most beautiful, chaotic woman I've ever met. There's no escaping me now." Kissing her again, she tries to wrap her arms around my neck, whimpering in pain as she pulls back.

Tears rim her eyes again. "I can't even fucking hug you." She begins to cry, and I feel helpless, knowing rest is the only thing that will help her heal.

"Hey, little one. Don't cry. Everything will be okay." Wiping her tears away, I kiss her forehead. "It's going to take time and a lot of rest. We have all the time in the world, baby."

She nods, and even though I know she feels defeated, her tears stop.

"Are you in pain? Do you want me to call the nurse?"

She shakes her head. "I hate pain meds. They make me feel like shit when they wear off."

"Savannah, if you're in pain, you need to take them."

She sighs. "Okay."

Pushing the call button on the side of the bed, the nurse comes in.

"She's in pain." I say in greeting.

She looks to Savannah, and she nods. The nurse disappears without another word, returning a few moments later with pain medication.

She swallows it with water and the nurse smiles at her, glaring at me before leaving.

Savannah giggles. "Can you lay with me?"

I'd give anything to wrap my arms around her right now, but her wound is in a delicate area. "I can't, little one. I'll hurt you."

"No you won't." She maneuvers her body to the other side slowly, making room for me.

Cursing under my breath, the temptation is too much, and I slide in beside her, her good side pressed against me. I can't wrap my arm around her, so I lay one hand on her thigh and the other above her head, running my fingers through her hair.

"I love you, Dex. I couldn't leave you. I had to come back." She whispers, holding my gaze.

"I love you too, baby. I'll never let you go."
Kissing her temple, my lips linger for a while.

Soon, her soft breathing fills the quiet room and I doze off to the sound of her doped up little snores.

Chapter Twenty-Four

Savannah

I feel like shit.

I've been awake for a few minutes, but I can't find the strength to open my eyes.

My head is throbbing, no doubt the side effects of the pain medication.

I guess a migraine is a small price to pay considering I have a damn bullet hole in my side.

I've been laying here, soaking in Dex's warmth, listening to his breathing.

When I woke up after surgery, I thought I was dreaming at first, seeing him next to me.

I fought.

I survived.

In the end, that's all that matters.

He stirs beside me, and I grit my teeth, scrunching my eyes closed as his arm comes up to wrap around my middle.

Shit.

This is going to hurt.

But he stops before his arm makes contact and I sigh in relief. Opening my eyes, he's watching me, his brows furrowed. "You were going to let me hurt you instead of waking me up? What if I wouldn't have woken up and stopped myself?"

His hand goes to the safe zone on my thigh, and I grip it tightly. "I'd rather feel pain than not feel your touch."

He groans, his fingers pressing into the soft flesh of my leg. "You can't say things like that to me right now."

"Why?" I ask, confused.

"It makes me want to fuck you so hard. I want to be the only one that causes you pain."

Quirking an eyebrow, I ask, "You want to hurt me, Archer?"

He groans again, closing his eyes. "So fucking bad, little one. I want to spank your ass until you cry and destroy your tight little pussy."

I gasp, and while it shouldn't be possible in my current state, my body lights up, desperate to have him inside me. "Dex, you're killing me." I moan as his hand slides under my hospital gown.

He buries his face in my neck, licking and nipping the sensitive skin there. "You need to come, baby? Will sliding my fingers inside your wet cunt make you feel better?"

"God, yes!" I hiss as his finger circles my swollen clit.

I've never been so grateful to be panty less.

"Be a good girl and don't make a sound." He licks the shell of my ear, pushing two fingers inside me. Biting my bottom lip to suppress a moan, he smiles against my skin. "That's my girl."

His pace is torturous and without thinking, I lift my hips, wincing as pain shoots through my side.

He stops immediately, searching my face. "Are you okay?"

"Please don't stop. I'll stay still, I promise."

He watches me for a few moments and as if he's testing me, he thrusts his fingers deeper and I whimper.

"Don't move and I'll give you what you need." He whispers against my ear, and I nod.

His thumb circles my clit as his fingers move inside me, finding the sweet spot that always makes me fall apart. Curling his fingers, I turn my head, sinking my teeth into his neck to stop myself from screaming.

"Jesus." He growls, his hand working my pussy faster and harder.

My legs begin to shake, my inner walls clenching around him.

"That's it, baby. Let go. Forget about everything but me inside you." He breathes, his tongue licking a trail up my neck, across my cheek before devouring my mouth.

My body obeys him, giving in to the carnal pleasure only he can give me.

On reflex, my body tries to arch off the bed, but he rises over me, his free hand wrapping around my throat, holding me in place.

He keeps his weight off me, pinning me by my throat and my pussy. The orgasm hits me hard, but he swallows my moans, his mouth taking everything I give.

My body finally relaxes, and he lies down, sliding his fingers out of me, sucking them into his mouth. "You're the best fucking thing I've ever tasted."

"Dex." I pant, wanting his cock so bad I think I'll die without it.

"I know, little one. Believe me, I want to sink inside you, feel you wrapped around me while I fuck you through this bed."

"You're not helping, asshole." I pout.

He chuckles, but it dies in his throat as I move my hand over his hard cock. It's tenting his loose sweatpants and my mouth waters as an idea comes to mind.

"You know, my mouth isn't injured. I could help you with that."

He groans. "You're a gorgeous, evil fucking woman." Squeezing his cock harder, he grunts, but pulls my hand away. "No, baby. We'll come back to this when you're better."

Giving him my best pouty face, he grins, kissing me slowly.

The door bursts open and we break apart.

"There she is, awake and cute as ever!" Rage singsongs and I laugh, wincing at the pain in my side.

She walks over to my bed, concern in her eyes. "Do you want a hug or a hand squeeze? Some kind of comfort?"

Jase's shoulders shake as he silently laughs behind her, and Dex smothers a grin as he gets out of the bed.

"Um, sure?" I reply hesitantly.

She leans down, embracing me gently and

patting the top of my head awkwardly. I feel like a golden retriever, but I know Rage is out of her comfort zone here.

She releases me as she straightens her posture, a rare show of emotion playing across her face. "Thank you for saving my life, Savannah."

Reaching out, I squeeze her hand with a reassuring smile. "Anytime, Rage."

Looking at Jase, he moves forward, laying a hand on my shoulder. "Thank you, sweet girl. You saved my life, too."

Tears burn my eyes, and he steps back, sharing an intimate look with his wife.

She wraps her arm around his waist, facing me once again. "So, does this mean we're friends?"

"I think so?" It comes out as a question.

"Don't get all shy on me now, Chaos. You're a savage bitch and we should definitely hang out. I'm warning you now though, I'm not really a wine and cheese kind of girl. I like weapons, strong alcohol, and sugar."

"Guns, beer and cookies?" I counter.

"Oh! Knives, margaritas and danish!" She spins around, facing our men who are doing a shit job hiding their amusement.

"Okay boys. A friendship has blossomed from the flames of madness. Jase let's go so they can have some time together." She waves awkwardly over her shoulder. "See ya later, buddy!"

The door closes as they leave, and I stare at it blankly, wondering what in the hell just happened.

Dex pushes himself off the wall, coming to the side of my bed. "You're so fucked, little one."

"Why?"

He quirks an eyebrow. "You're besties with a loyal, protective hit woman who has never had a friend before. You're in for it."

"Hmmm, I also belong to a deadly, protective hit man who's scary as hell when I'm in danger."

"You're damn right and you'd do well to remember it. You have three people who will protect you at all costs, but one of them is madly fucking in love with you."

"Dex."

"Yeah, baby?"

"I love you, too."

Chapter Twenty-Five

Declan

"I want a machete, too." Savannah says out of nowhere and I laugh.

"Where did that come from?" I ask.

"The night I got shot, I looked, and you were wielding a fucking machete."

"Yeah. The angrier I am, the more damage I do." I grimace and she smiles.

She's fucking perfect.

"I see that. So, do I get one too?"

"Sure, baby. I'll get you one." I promise and she claps her hands together excitedly.

She's been home from the hospital for a week. She's healing well even though she's stubborn as hell and doesn't listen to a damn word I say.

Rage made good on her promise the other day, bringing strawberry danish and *virgin* margaritas. Savannah looked at her like she was crazy, but Rage said, "Alcohol isn't good for you while you're healing."

Little chaos got her first dose of mama bear and us boys thoroughly enjoyed it. She grumbled the entire time Rage fussed over her. She finally perked up when she bit into the danish.

Storm is pissed off because Savannah can't get on the floor and love all over him. With her lying in the bed recovering, all he can do is plant his front two paws on the side of the mattress and she hangs her hand off the side, petting his head. She begged me to put him in bed with her, but I refused. He's like a wrecking ball and I don't want him to accidentally hurt her.

Jase and I patched up the rental, saving the move to our new home for when Savannah is recovered.

I wanted to bring in a preacher to marry us, but she insisted she be able to stand while getting married.

The click of the button on the remote breaks me away from my thoughts. Glancing at her, she looks bored, clicking the button over and over, flipping through the channels.

She huffs in annoyance, and I grin. "Baby."

"Yeah?" She responds absentmindedly, still clicking the damn remote.

"Talk to me."

She tosses the remote on the bed, sighing dramatically. "If I have to lay in this bed one more second, I'm going to die of boredom."

Her exaggerated expression makes me chuckle and I turn onto my side to face her. "What can I do to keep you occupied, little one?"

Her lips tug up at the corners and it dawns on me how I walked straight into that one. "You have a big, pierced cock I need to get reacquainted with."

It's been torture, not being able to slide inside her body the way I crave to. I've missed her warmth, her touch, and the way she feels wrapped around me. I haven't touched her intimately since that night in the hospital for fear of hurting her. It's taking every ounce of control I have, but her wellbeing will always come first.

"Savannah, you need to heal first." I say gently, knowing this is hard for her too.

"I understand, Dex. Can you do me a favor?" She smiles sweetly.

I nod. "Anything."

"Can you go buy me a vibrator? I'd do it myself, but I'm bedridden."

My eyebrows shoot to my hairline, my jaw dropping.

She's lost her fucking mind if she thinks I'm going to buy her a vibrator with my rock-hard cock right here waiting. "No."

She manages to suppress her victorious smile as I fall into her trap again. "Why not, big guy?"

Rising from the mattress, I hover above her, holding my weight on my forearms. "You have no fucking idea how badly I want to sink my cock inside your tight cunt. I'm holding back because you're hurt. You can be angry with me all you like, but it won't change the fact we'll both suffer until you're healed."

Her smile fades, replaced with understanding, but the longing is still there, and I know it's a reflection of what she sees when she looks at me. "Yes." She whispers.

"Now that we're on the same page, I'm going to eat your pussy while you scream my name."

She gasps as I kiss her hard before crawling

down her body. She spreads her legs as far as she can without stretching enough to cause any pain. Pushing her t-shirt to her waist, my mouth waters as I lean in, inhaling her intoxicating scent.

My tongue darts out, licking her swollen clit. Her sweet flavor bursts across my tongue and my control snaps.

Fuck, I've missed this.

Gripping the backs of her knees, I spread her legs wider, and she doesn't complain. Plunging my tongue inside her, she moans, her fingers tugging my hair. Her body trembles and I know she's fighting the urge to buck against my face.

I'm proud of her, so I reward her control by thrusting two fingers deep inside her soaked pussy, sucking her clit between my lips.

She cries out as she clenches around me and my cock throbs against my pants. Scraping my teeth across her clit sets her off and she screams my name, her hips lifting off the bed as her control shatters.

Without stopping, I drag every ounce of pleasure from her body and it's not until she's a few inches off the mattress before she winces, lowering herself back down.

"You okay?" I ask, crawling back up her body.

"Yeah." She pants, trying to catch her breath. Kissing her deeply, she moans as she tastes herself. "I really want your dick in my mouth." She breathes against my lips.

"You're killing me, little one." I groan, rolling

onto my side, adjusting my painfully hard cock.

"Please? I know I can't bend to do it, but I really want you on top, fucking my face."

"Christ." How the fuck do I refuse that?

"Come on. You've tasted me over and over. It's my turn." She slowly slides down the bed, no sign of discomfort as I watch her face closely.

Sliding my pants off, I reach behind me, pulling my shirt over my head. Straddling her chest, I look down at her, giving her time to change her mind.

Her pupils blow wide as she takes in my cock, licking her lips unconsciously.

"Look at me." She meets my gaze. "Tap my thigh if it's too much and everything stops." She nods. "I'm serious, Savannah. One fucking twinge of pain and you tap out."

"Okay."

My hand grips the headboard for support, as the other strokes my cock leisurely. She's in a trance, her lips parted, watching me intently.

"Give it to me, Dex. Now." She demands.

"Open your mouth and stick out your tongue."

She does as she's told, and I grit my teeth as I slide myself between her lips, the warmth of her mouth nothing short of perfection.

She closes her lips around me, flicking her tongue over the head, tasting the precum leaking from the slit. She moans, the vibration making my eyes roll back in my head. Her tongue traces the vein on my shaft and my other hand comes up to grip the headboard.

She's watching me, and it makes me harder. "Fuck, Savannah. You're taking me so well."

Hollowing her cheeks, she sucks me hard, bobbing her head up and down.

This won't do.

"Don't move. I'll feed you my cock." Her eyes widen and I smirk.

I drop one hand to her face, tracing her top lip, loving how tight it is from being stretched around my cock. "Shield your teeth from my piercings, baby."

She nods and I grab the headboard with both hands again, pushing inside her mouth. She gags and the contraction of her throat muscles feel so fucking good. "Relax your throat. Let me in."

She whimpers and I repeat the action, but she gags again, tears leaking from the corners of her eyes. "You're so fucking gorgeous choking on my cock." Pushing and pulling slowly, my hips jerk the first time I slide all the way down her throat, and she doesn't gag. "Fuck. Remember to tap out if it's too much."

Sinking deeper inside her mouth, the headboard creaks under my grip. This is her first-time sucking cock, but she's a fucking pro.

It feels like lightning shooting down my spine, my balls drawing tight. I'm about to embarrass myself, but I don't give a damn. "I'm about to come, baby. Where do you want it?"

She tightens her lips around me, and I'm done. "Swallow every drop." I growl, fucking her throat until my climax hits. Two more thrusts and I roar her name, shooting my cum down her throat. She swallows greedily, not letting go until she licks every drop from my shaft.

I've needed her so badly this past week and fuck did she deliver.

Sliding out of her mouth, I roll to my side of the bed, trying to catch my breath. She's doing the same, but I feel her stare.

Turning my head, she's smiling, and it makes me hard again. "You should definitely taste yourself."

Leaning in, I crash our lips together, tasting myself on her tongue. "We taste good." I groan against her mouth.

She whimpers, tugging my hand between her legs.

Fucking drenched.

"Sucking my cock make you wet, little one?"

"Yes." She hisses as I push two fingers inside her.

I make her come over and over until she passes out.

She needs her rest because as soon as she's healed and my cock slips inside her, she'll be trapped in this bed for days.

Opening my eyes, I stretch my arms above my head. Glancing at Savannah's side of the bed, she isn't there.

Jumping from the bed, I yell her name as I rush

through the small rental house. "Savannah!"

"In here!" She calls from the kitchen.

Turning the corner, she's standing at the counter, a mug of coffee in her hand.

Stalking towards her, I lift her shirt quickly, checking her wound.

It looks good.

We're able to leave the bandages off now since it's healing well, but I'm still worried.

She swats at my hands. "Dex, I'm fine."

"Why are you out of bed? I told you to wake me up if you need anything and I'll get it for you." She rolls her eyes, making my cock twitch.

"You're a psychopath. I've been home for two weeks. The bandages are gone and I'm healing perfectly fine."

Stealing the coffee from her hand, I place it on the counter beside me. Her breaths come quicker as I invade her space, not leaving an inch between us. "Oh baby, you have no idea just how psycho I can be when it comes to you." Her eyes widen and I continue. "You're mine, Savannah. Your safety comes first, and I will do *anything* to ensure that."

She grins. "You're *my* psycho, Declan Archer."

"You're my fucking world, little chaos. Never forget, I'll destroy anything and everything that tries to come between us." I kiss her deeply and she melts against me.

She hums, grinning against my lips. "I want a tattoo."

The sudden change in topic has me pulling

away. "Really? What do you want?"

"The chaos symbol, like my necklace."

Cupping her face in my palms, I kiss the corner of her mouth. "Where?"

"Over the bullet hole when it heals. I know it'll scar, which I don't mind, but I think the tattoo is fitting."

"I like it." I agree, excited my girl wants some ink. "You'll go to my artist, and we'll set something up once your healed."

She bounces on her toes. "I would say you can get one with me, but I don't think you have any skin left."

"I'll get one. I have room on my neck."

"Neck tattoos are sexy. What are you going to get?" She smirks, trailing her finger down the side of my neck.

"Your lips."

She laughs. "What? How?"

"You're going to put on your favorite lipstick and kiss a piece of paper. They'll trace it and tattoo it on my neck."

She smiles. "That's the sweetest thing I've ever heard."

"Nah. The sweetest thing you've ever heard is we're getting married tomorrow. You're walking now, so it's time to make you mine, legally."

She gasps, blinking rapidly, tears trailing down her face. "Dex."

"Mrs. Archer." I smirk, wrapping my arms around her shoulders.

Marrying Savannah is the ultimate gift. I don't deserve her, and I never will, but I'll spend my life making sure she doesn't regret giving me her heart.

She sniffles, laying her head on my chest. "Just for the record, I would've said yes if you would've asked."

"I know." I say, kissing the top of her head.

She laughs and the sound feeds my soul, just like the woman in my arms.

Chapter Twenty-Six

Savannah

"I have to find a job." I groan, rolling onto my back.

We got married two days ago and we haven't left this bed since. I told Dex we weren't getting married unless he gave me a proper wedding night.

That got his attention.

It had been weeks since we were intimate, and I couldn't take it anymore.

We ended up waiting another two weeks before getting married.

Just to make sure.

He even took me for another checkup just to ensure I was cleared to have sex. The doctor said I'm healing nicely and as long as I'm comfortable, there's no reason why we can't.

So, after our little ceremony that included a minister, Jase, and Rage, he gave me an entire night of slow, passionate love-making that made me want to scream in ecstasy one minute and cry the next.

Our souls melded together that night.

I didn't think it was possible to love him more than I already did, but he blew that theory out of the water.

"About that-" He starts but I cut him off.

Rolling onto my side, I glare at him. "Declan,

we agreed that I'd go back to work after everything blew over."

"You are going back to work." He states simply and I stare at him expectantly, waiting for him to continue. "You're going to work with me."

"Killing people?" My eyes widen.

"The correct term is hitwoman." He grumbles.

"You want me to come and work with you?"

"Why not? You're good at killing people and I want you with me all the time."

Staring at him blankly for a few moments, processing the offer, I hate myself when hurt flashes across his face.

"You don't want to work with me?" His jaw clenches.

My chest cracks open and I regret my silence immediately.

I love Dex more than life itself and what girl doesn't want to spend every moment with her hitman husband?

I sure the fuck do.

Rising from the mattress, I crawl on top of him, scraping my nails through the stubble on his face. He closes his eyes, groaning as my fingers move back and forth.

Bending down, I kiss him softly. "I do want to work with you. I want to be with you all day, every day. I just needed a second to process being a killer for a living."

Suddenly, he flips me onto my back, pinning my hands above my head. I've lost count how many orgasms he's given me since yesterday. My limp body is exhausted, but just when I think I have nothing left to give, he does this shit, bringing me back to life.

Trailing his nose down my neck, I moan, needing him all over again. "You want to be with me all the time, little savage? Every day we'll wake up together. Eat together. Kill together. Every night I'll fuck you senseless, just to do it all over again the next day. And every day after that, until we're old and gray."

Arching into him, a whimper escapes my throat. "That's exactly what I want."

"Of course it is. Do you know why?" He whispers against my ear.

I can't find my voice when he makes me feel like this. All I can do is shake my head.

"Because you're all fucking mine. Only mine. Forever all eternity. Isn't that right, wife?"

Jesus.

"I'm yours. Only yours." I'm panting and he smiles against my cheek.

"That's right. Now, be a good girl and let me fuck my gorgeous wife so I can cook her dinner while she naps."

I grin. "Do your worst, husband."

He kisses me softly before licking and nipping his way down my throat. He pauses at my breasts, sucking a hard nipple between his lips, letting his teeth graze across the sensitive bud. The sensation sends a million electric shocks across my skin.

Gripping his dark hair between my fingers, I tug hard as he switches to my other breast, his hot mouth ravaging my aching nipple. My back arches, pushing me further into his mouth and he groans in approval.

He releases my nipple with a pop, grinning wickedly as he works his mouth down my body. He reaches the apex of my thighs, breathing deeply as his eyes drift closed. His expression is hungry, and it sends tingles to my aching core.

"Dex, please."

"Please what, baby?" He smirks and I want to smack his smug ass. He knows exactly what he's doing.

"Eat my pussy." I hiss and the victorious look on his face is sexy as fuck before he dives in, giving me exactly what I want.

Pushing two fingers inside my drenched pussy, he sucks my clit into his mouth, his teeth nipping me with a sting of delicious pain. Pleasure coils in my lower belly and it always shocks me just how quickly he can make me come.

My hips rise and fall in rhythm with his sinful mouth, and just as I'm about to explode, he stops.

"Dex!" I whine, chasing his mouth as he pulls away.

"You're going to come on my cock." He growls, crawling over my body.

He positions the head of his cock at my opening and before I can take another breath, he slams inside me, stilling as he bumps my cervix.

His name is ripped from my throat as I claw at his shoulders, pulling him down on top of me. His arms snake beneath me, pinning me against his large body.

We cling to each other, only our hips moving as we grind against each other. He feels so fucking good, tears leak from the corners of my eyes.

"Your tears are fucking beautiful when they're caused by my cock." He groans, licking the salty emotion from my cheeks.

I'm teetering on the edge of oblivion, my body ready to burst into flames from my husband's measured control. My pussy contracts with every deep stroke until I finally ignite, burning to ashes beneath my handsome sex demon.

Crying out his name over and over, he stills inside me, moaning as he fills me to the brim with his warm release. We hold onto each other like the world will tear us apart if we let go.

He rolls onto his side without breaking our connection, hiking my thigh over his hip while he's still inside me. He grips my ass possessively, taking my mouth in a hypnotic kiss that makes my toes curl.

"You're my life and you'll be my death, Mrs. Archer." He whispers against my lips.

"You'll be my life and I'll follow you in death, Mr. Archer."

We spend quiet moments gazing at each other, lost in our own little bubble.

His hand trails up my side, over my chest until

he reaches my face. He tucks a few loose strands of hair behind my ear before cupping my cheek in his palm. "Sleep, sweet girl."

Chapter Twenty-Seven

Declan

"We should get leather vests and have patches made!" Rage announces and I pinch the bridge of my nose, the vein in Jase's forehead throbbing.

"Oh! Mine will say 'Chaos' and yours can say 'Killer'." Savannah chimes in and I'm reminded once again why I love this fucking woman so much.

Rage looks to Jase, quirking an eyebrow. "What do you think?"

Scrubbing his hand down his face, he sighs. "Rage, we're assassins. We're supposed to stay hidden, not advertise we kill people."

She glares, and I wait for her to tear into him, but my wife interrupts. "Rage, we can get tattoos!"

The suggestion saves Jase's ass and I see the relief as his eyes dart to mine. Smirking at him, he flips me off, a grin tugging at his lips.

Clapping my hands together, the girls turn my way. "Tattoos it is then." I agree, ready for this conversation to be over.

Besides, I like the idea of Savannah's smooth skin being covered in ink.

Rage pulls out her phone, texting our tattoo artist, setting up an appointment for the day after tomorrow. I have my own little surprise, something guaranteed to make them happy.

"We have a new job." I interrupt and their focus

turns back to me. Jase smiles knowingly.

"Hell yes! I'm finally healed and ready to start." Savannah chimes in, bouncing on her toes.

Her wound is healed, only a little tenderness when pressure is applied to the area.

"Spit it out, Dex." Rage quips and I chuckle.

One word is all I have to say. "Twins."

Rage gasps, absolute shock rendering her speechless.

That's new.

Jase grins, pulling her into his arms. "Are you happy, baby?"

"We're finally going after the Delaney brothers?" She asks with hope in her eyes.

He nods. "It's time. They're all yours."

"Who are the Delaney brothers?" Savannah questions and I keep quiet, letting Rage fill her in.

She hates them more than any other mark we've had. She's wanted to kill them for months, but we needed more intel.

"They're fucking monsters, Chaos. Their mother should've swallowed them or at least taken a plan b. They don't deserve the air they breathe, and I can't wait to watch them take their last."

Savannah's eyes widen and I chuckle. "Do you remember the news story a while back about the girls found in the land fill?"

She nods and Rage continues. "Those motherfuckers kidnap underage girls, chain them in a basement, and charge sadistic fucks a fee to torture and rape them. Once the girls are too damaged for a profit, they offer their death to the highest bidder. Fucking people pay the brothers to kill the poor girls. After they're dead, they dump them at the landfill. Their families never know what happened to them."

Savannah doesn't move.

She doesn't blink.

She stares at Rage, and they seem to have a silent conversation.

That's fucking scary.

I glance at Jase and his expression says he agrees with me.

"Let's go out to dinner." Rage announces, leaving me and Jase confused.

He shrugs his shoulders, and we lock up, following the girls out to the truck.

Planning a double murder has them starving all of the sudden.

"What time did they say they'd be back?" I ask Jase.

After dinner last night, Rage and Savannah told us they wanted to have a girl's night out. I figured they'd wait until this weekend, but they wanted to go out tonight.

"They didn't." He replies, his brows furrowed.

"They're planning something. What do you think it is?"

He sighs. "Fuck if I know. You should check the tracker."

"You know she hates it when I do that." I groan and he grins.

"But you do it anyway."

True.

I check the tracking app multiple times whenever she's out of my sight. It's not that I don't trust her, I need to know where she is at all times. I never recovered from Colin kidnapping her. She thought I was protective before, but I'm a full-on wife stalker now.

Pulling my phone from my pocket, I tap my foot, waiting for the app to load. As the little dot comes into view, my heart stops.

"Fuck!" I yell, jumping to my feet.

Jase follows suit. "Where the fuck are they?"

"The Lion's Den." I growl.

They're in the club the Delaney brothers own.

Without us.

Without protection.

Get ready, little one. You're in fucking trouble now.

"Let's go!" Jase barks just as a text comes through on his phone, then mine.

Wife: Hurry and bring rope. The Lion's Den. Don't be mad.

Me: On our way. Mad doesn't even come close.

Wife: You'll see when you get here. Drive around back.

Me: Your ass is mine for this little stunt. I'm going to enjoy every second of it.

Wife: **Me too.**

Brat.

"She told me to drive around back and bring rope." I say, backing out of the driveway.

"I'm going to redden Rage's ass for whatever the hell they're up to. You should do the same." He grits out, his fist clenched in his lap.

I nod in agreement. "Believe me, she'll be punished."

The drive is quiet as we both seethe, working out how to handle our women taking matters into their own hands. They both knew we'd never let them do this alone. I admire their independence, but they've put their lives at risk. Not only the risk of death, but torture and violation.

The club comes into view, and I pull down the back alley, turning off my headlights. Coming to a stop by the dumpster, the yellow streetlight shines brightly enough to illuminate a strange scene.

Two men lay on the ground, unmoving while Rage and Savannah stand over them casually. They smile broadly when they see us, having no idea just how pissed we are.

What the fuck?

Jase and I jump out of the truck, and as we get closer, I realize who is laying on the ground.

The Delaney brothers.

My eyes snap to Savannah who has the fucking audacity to wave like we're meeting for a damn coffee date.

Before I have a chance to speak, Jase starts in. "Explain."

Rage squares her shoulders, lifting her chin. "We need to tie them up and load them in the back of the truck. I'll explain on the way to the warehouse."

His chest rumbles. "You two get in the truck, now."

They actually listen, not saying a word as they do what they're told. The doors close and I reach into the bed of the truck, pulling out the rope.

Handing a roll to Jase, we hog tie the pieces of shit and load them into the bed, one at a time. Closing the tailgate, we climb inside the cab, the girls staying silent in the back. Speeding from the alleyway, I head towards the warehouse.

"Jase-" Rage starts but he doesn't let her finish.

"What happened to not doing jobs alone?" He seethes and I don't think I've ever seen him this mad at her.

Don't get me wrong, I'm pissed, but I'm more relieved they're okay. I'll have to think about how to handle this later. Right now, we need to deal with the situation at hand.

"We're not doing it alone. Savannah and I handled the first part of the job discreetly and then we called you." She shoots back, not at all bothered by his tone.

"Bullshit! You know this isn't how we work. We do the entire job together or not at all." He fumes.

This shit is escalating quickly.

I'm fully expecting Rage to flip her shit, but she surprises me. Climbing into the front, she straddles Jase's lap, cupping his face in her palms. His body is rigid as he stares at her. "This was the only way, baby. We needed to lure them away so we could trap them. I've thought about it for months and I knew you'd never go along with me going in alone. Chaos offered to help, and I knew between the two of us, we'd get it done." She leans in, kissing his cheek. "I'd never put myself in danger if I didn't think I could handle it. I wouldn't risk Savannah's life either. I knew we could do this. Don't be upset with me, please."

She kisses him and I see the moment he relents out of the corner of my eye. His body deflates as he wraps his arms around her, crushing her against him.

"I can't fucking lose you." He whispers and I glance in the rearview mirror, meeting Savannah's gaze.

She mouths 'I love you' and that's all it takes for my anger to dissipate.

We reach the warehouse, Jase and Rage hopping out first.

"Stay." I grit out, exiting the front, immediately opening the back door and climbing inside.

She doesn't move, waiting to see what I'll do.

My hand darts out, wrapping around her throat, pulling her into my lap. She comes willingly, straddling my hips, her arms looping around my neck.

"Are you sorry?" I ask, tightening my hold around her throat.

"No." She smirks and my fingers flex against her soft skin.

While her answer angers me, a sense of pride swells in my chest, the woman she's become a vast contrast to the lonely, depressed girl I met not so long ago. I love both versions, but that smile of hers brings me to my knees.

And once I'm on my knees, I'll worship my chaotic queen in every way possible.

"Will you do it again?"

She nods. "If I have to."

Fuck me.

What am I going to do with her? "Tell me next time?"

"Will you let me do it if I do?"

"I need to know you're safe, Savannah." I hold her gaze, letting her see the truth.

You're my world and I'm nothing without you.

She pulls at my wrist, and I release her throat as she lunges forward, kissing me like her life depends on it. She forces her tongue between my lips, and I open eagerly, desperate to taste her sweet flavor. My hands grip her ass, and she moans into my mouth, grinding down on my hard cock.

The world fades around us.

I forget about Rage and Jase.

About the Delaney brothers.

I lose myself in my wife. The reason I breathe. The reason my heart beats. The reason my soul burns.

Until Rage knocks on the window.

Savannah pulls away, huffing with annoyance. Opening the door, she climbs out, gripping my hand, pulling me out too. Wrapping an arm around her waist, I crush her to me. "I love you, baby." I whisper against her ear and her body shudders.

"I love you, husband."

"That's so sweet, but we need to hurry before the sedatives wear off." Rage interrupts.

We get to work, unloading the jackasses, bringing them into the warehouse. Tying them each to a beam, we all grab a chair, sitting and waiting for them to wake up.

"I need details." I say, looking at the girls who share a secret smile.

"It was so easy!" Savannah beams and I can't help but chuckle.

"We went in looking hot, drew their attention, asked them to follow us out back for a quickie, stabbed them with syringes full of sedatives and called you." Rage explains.

My hackles rise, my eyes meeting Savannah's. "Did they fucking touch you?"

She shakes her head vehemently as Rage cringes. "Ew. No."

My jaw unclenches, my body relaxing. Gripping Savannah's wrist, I tug her from her chair. She straddles my lap, and we wrap our arms around each other. Burying my face in her neck, I breathe her in, knowing this is the calm before the storm.

While I'd love to rip these two motherfuckers from limb to limb, the girls want them. And I'll do anything to make my girl smile.

Groans and whimpers pull our attention to the assholes on the floor.

Savannah shifts in my lap, a sadistic smile spreading across her face. "Hello boys."

Chapter Twenty-Eight

Savannah

Our men tied the Delaney brothers to the beams in the center of the warehouse.

Once I assured Dex they didn't touch me, he calmed down so Rage and I can have the honors.

They're slowly waking up, their heads lolling from side to side, looking helpless and terrified.

Jonas, the one missing a good chunk of his right ear, is mumbling incoherently as we all stand in silence.

Ricky groans, his tongue licking his dry lips.

"Which one do you want, Chaos?" Rage asks, her eyes trained on our play toys.

"Jonas." I quip, staring at the helpless maggot, smirking as he struggles to focus.

"Why him?" Dex questions curiously.

"I overheard a conversation at the club earlier. Apparently, one of the girls he kidnapped bit off most of his ear."

Rage cackles beside me, Jase looking at her with pride. "That's why his ear looks like an asshole?" She steps closer to him, leaning down to thump it with her finger. He moans loudly as she stares at the deformed appendage. "Still tender, I see."

Dex watches me as I move in between Jonas's legs, squatting down so I'm eye level with him.

"I'm going to enjoy every second of this. Your screams. Your tears. Your pain. The only thing sweeter will be when I dump your lifeless body at the landfill."

A strong hand grips my bicep, jerking me to my feet. Dex spins me around, backing me against the wall, knocking the breath from my lungs. His large frame pins me in place as his fingers grip my chin, forcing my gaze to his. "The heat in your eyes and the fire in your words have my cock so fucking hard." He grinds himself against me and I'm instantly soaked.

"Fuck me." I moan, desperate to be stretched and filled by his big cock.

"Christ, Savannah." He groans, picking me up, my arms and legs wrapping around his large frame. He pulls me from the wall, carrying me to the small room in the back of the warehouse. He sits me on the desk, pulling me to the edge by my thighs. "This is going to be fast and hard."

"I'm counting on it."

His hands slide up my dress, groaning as he sees the knife strapped to my thigh. Gripping my thong, he snatches the material down my legs. Reaching for him, I unbuckle his belt quickly, barely getting his pants unbuttoned before he shoves them down. He lines himself up with my opening, slamming inside with such force, my ass slides across the desk. A scream erupts from my throat, but his mouth is on mine before the sound travels through the warehouse.

"Don't let go of me." He growls against my lips, setting a brutal pace.

My head falls back, lost in the pain and pleasure of Dex's glorious cock. He takes me to new heights every time we're together like this. Just when I think it can't possibly get any better, he shows me how terribly wrong I am.

"Dex, you're so deep." I cry out, his hips rolling so I feel every piercing dragging along my walls.

"This is where I belong. Inside you. Claiming every inch of your body." His chest rumbles, the sound plunging me into the deepest sea of pleasure.

He pulls out to the tip, slamming inside me over and over until the fraying thread holding my sanity together finally snaps. I scream his name, my nails digging into his back, the warmth of his blood coating my fingertips.

His body tenses as he roars my name, crushing our bodies together until there's no beginning or end. He fills me with his warm cum as we struggle to catch our breath.

His forearms catch his weight as he collapses on top of me. "I'm going to enjoy watching you kill him with my cum leaking down your thighs."

"Me too." I whisper, my throat raw from screaming his name.

His cock twitches inside me and I gasp, ready to go again.

"Later." He groans, and we both wince as he pulls out of me.

I've always hated this part. To become one and experience euphoria only for it to end. I love having him inside me, so close we survive on each other's breaths. Our souls joining in the ultimate connection.

He must sense my thoughts. "I'd live inside you if I could. Keep my cock locked inside your warm pussy every second of the day." He smirks. "But I don't think we'd get much accomplished."

Huffing out a laugh, I take his hand as he helps me from the desk. "Come on, big guy. We have shit to do, people to kill."

After adjusting our clothes, we head back to the others, walking hand in hand. As the Delaney brothers come into view, I stifle a giggle. Rage is humming a song I've never heard, her boot covered foot tapping in rhythm on Ricky's balls. Jase is standing off to the side, a smile tugging at his lips.

"Come on Chaos! I'm feeling stabby." Rage whines and I let go of Dex's hand, skipping my way over beside her.

Kneeling between Jonas's legs, his eyes widen as I pull the knife from the sheath attached to my thigh. "My blade will look so pretty covered in your blood." Gripping his shirt, I slice through the fabric easily. "I'll have revenge for all the girls you raped and murdered."

Pressing the tip of the blade above his right nipple, I flick my wrist in one smooth motion, slicing the hard nub from his chest.

He screams in agony as Jase and Dex squirm, Rage cheering beside me. "I wish I had pom poms for this shit!"

Her excitement is contagious, and I smile.

Now the first blood has been drawn, and I hyperfocus on my target, the rest of the room fading away. I never thought I'd be one for torture, but as I slice off Jonas's other nipple, I'm finding that I thoroughly enjoy it.

Blood trickles down his torso and I watch the trail disappear beneath the waistband of his pants. Unsnapping his jeans, I jerk them down to his knees, his small, flaccid dick staring at me like a worm peeking through the dirt.

He whimpers helplessly, pulling against his restraints. "You won't get away with this, bitch!"

Before I can respond, a black boot connects with Jonas's face, a crunch sounding as blood sprays from his mouth. "Watch your fucking mouth, *bitch*."

Glancing up at Dex, his jaw is clenched, the murderous energy surrounding him cocooning me with his love and protection.

Reaching for his fist, his fingers unclench, relaxing at my touch. His eyes snap to mine and his expression softens. "Sorry, little chaos. Please continue." Bringing his fingers to my lips, I kiss them softly, and he smiles, stepping back to give me room.

Giving my attention back to Jonas, he looks utterly pathetic as blood and drool leak from his mouth. I don't speak before gripping his sad cock in my hand, slicing through it smoothly with my blade. His gurgling screams fill the room, but I silence him quickly, stuffing the useless appendage inside his mouth.

Blood gushes from the wound, his muffled voice overshadowed by Jase's painful groan. "He deserved it, but fuck, that's brutal."

Rage chuckles beside him. "That's art, if you ask me."

Standing up slowly, my eyes are transfixed between Jonas's legs, a sense of peace coming over me knowing I've served a little justice for all the girls this prick has tortured and murdered.

A warm chest presses against my back, Dex's muscular arms wrapping around my waist. He places a soft kiss below my ear. "I'm so fucking proud of you, little one. Those girls can rest now."

Swallowing my emotion, I bend down, gripping Jonas's jaw until his mouth opens further. With two fingers, I push his cock deeper down his throat, smiling as he chokes.

Rot in hell, motherfucker.

I melt into Dex's embrace as we all watch the sick fuck struggle for air until his body finally gives out.

Spinning me around, Dex kisses me roughly, devouring my lips as I hold onto him tightly. He doesn't let up, stealing every breath I have. "You're so fucking beautiful embracing your darkness, little chaos. I love you covered in blood and full of my cum." He whispers against my lips. "You're my lifeforce, baby. Without you, I'm nothing."

I'm momentarily speechless, words unable to describe what I feel for this man. Gripping his dark hair, I tug gently until his gaze meets mine. "You brought me back to life, Declan. You gave me a reason to fight. You showed me how to live again. I'm yours in this life and the next."

He slams his lips to mine, our declarations mild compared to our feelings for each other.

There will never be anyone else for me.

Declan Archer is my husband, the keeper of my soul.

He's my partner in living life and bringing death.

We're so lost in each other, forgetting there's another asshole who needs to die.

Slowly pulling away, I glance across the room, realizing Rage has already killed her mark. His throat is cut, a pool of blood surrounding his lifeless body.

That's odd.

Rage usually likes to play with her prey.

She's disappeared, along with Jase and I smile when I hear her pleasure filled moans through the walls.

"Looks like blood and death makes us all horny." I laugh.

Dex chuckles, pulling me closer. "I never knew how beautiful it could be until I saw it on you."

"You're going soft, Archer."

He grinds his hard length against my hip. "You'll never have to worry about me being soft around you, baby."

Huffing out a laugh, I swat his chest. "Perv."

"Only for you, little chaos." He kisses me again before pulling me into an empty storage room, sitting me on top of a desk. "Now be a good little wife and let your husband fuck you senseless again."

Spreading my legs slowly, I grin. "Do your worst, husband."

Epilogue

One Year Later...

Savannah

Sitting in the woods by myself, fear and anticipation are a dizzying concoction in my veins.

The idea came to me a few days ago while I was trying to think of an anniversary gift for Dex.

We've been married for a year and my life has never been better.

My husband owns me, body, heart and soul.

We bought a beautiful home after we were married. It's an adorable, little cabin on the outskirts of town, not far from Jase and Rage.

Storm finally outgrew his destructive stage, no longer being a cute little menace. There's nothing little about my boy, anymore. At one-hundred and fifty pounds, he's more like a pony instead of a dog. Even at his weight, he still thinks he can sit in my lap.

Who am I to tell him no?

No matter how big he gets, he'll always be my baby.

Jase and Rage are our best friends, so all of us working together at the organization is a fucking blast.

Who wouldn't want to kill bad guys with their husband and best buddies?

My chest tightens, fear spiking my heart rate,

and it makes me smile.

It has nothing to do with being alone in the woods in the middle of the night.

It's because I disappeared later this afternoon and I've ignored all of Dex's calls and texts.

I've never taken off the necklace he gave me with the tracker, and tonight, it plays into my game.

We've always had an amazing sex life, but I figured I'd take things to the next level for our anniversary.

He's my beast.

The big bad predator.

Tonight, I want to be his helpless prey.

Limbs crack in the distance, heavy footsteps moving through the woods with purpose.

He's here.

My hands shake as I stand from the ground, leaning against a boulder, waiting for my pissed off husband to appear.

Squinting my eyes, his dark form comes into view, my thighs clenching together.

Fuck, I need him.

He comes closer and closer until his gaze collides with mine. The moonlight filters through the trees, and I catch glimpses of his clenched jaw and darkening eyes.

His anger beats against me as he approaches, his cold gaze making me nervous.

Shit.

I should've thought this through a little bit

more.

"What are you doing?" His calm voice unnerves me.

"Um, happy anniversary?" It comes out as a question instead of a confident statement.

His head tilts to the side. "You did this on purpose?"

"Yeah." I whisper, realizing my grand plan has all went to shit.

He grips my waist, spinning me around, pushing me against the boulder. "Do you want to play, little chaos?" He trails his lips down the side of my neck, goosebumps erupting across my skin.

My sensitive nipples harden painfully, my hips instinctively pushing back against him. "Yes." I breathe.

"Are you sure? I tracked you into these woods, not knowing what I would find. Do you know what that did to me, wife?"

His cool tone doesn't sit well with me, and guilt settles heavy in my chest. "I'm sorry. I was trying to surprise you."

He chuckles darkly. "You're the one who is going to be surprised."

"W-what do you mean?" I stutter, wondering if he's about to flip his shit.

"Run." He growls, taking a step back.

Without a moment's thought, I take off running through the woods.

I don't look back.

I don't slow down.

I run as fast as I can.

This is a side of Dex I've never seen.

I don't know what I expected, but this is so much better.

My legs slide easily against each other as I run, my arousal soaking my thighs. I'm wearing a short, gray sundress with no panties, meant for easy access.

I hear the creek in the distance, and I know exactly where I am. Before I can reach the water, strong arms wrap around my middle, pushing me against a tree. The bark scrapes my cheek, but the sting of pain only heightens my desire.

"Gotcha." He breathes against my ear, and I push my ass against his hard cock.

"What are you going to do with me?"

"I've hunted you. I've caught you. Now, I'm going to fuck you." He growls. "Get on your hands and knees."

Obeying him quickly, I drop to all fours, the short dress riding up my ass. His answering groan makes me grin.

His rough hands glide up my thighs, pushing my dress past my hips. "Fuck, you're soaked. Do you like being chased, little one?"

"Only by you." I moan as his fingers slide easily through my slick pussy lips.

The sound of him unbuckling his belt makes my hips sway. I'm desperate to have him inside me.

He takes his time before falling to his knees behind me and I gasp when his hard cock presses against my opening. "I hope you're ready." He growls, slamming inside me to the hilt.

His name is ripped from my lips, his piercings dragging along my inner walls as he sets a brutal pace. Digging my nails into the dirt, I'm grabbing for anything to hold me in place. His deep thrusts push me across the ground, twigs and rocks digging into my knees and palms.

His deep grunts behind me and his bruising grip on my waist has me tumbling over the edge, a powerful orgasm weakening my limbs and I collapse to the ground.

"Oh no you don't. We're nowhere near done." He groans, his palm pushing between my shoulders, the side of my face pressing into the dirt.

"More." I beg.

He gives me exactly what I ask for, using my body for his own pleasure. I'm nothing in this moment, only Dex's fuck toy and the thought sends a shiver down my spine.

The pressure between my shoulders eases as he readjusts his angle, but I break free from his grasp, flipping onto my back. He quirks an eyebrow, and I push his chest hard, successfully knocking him onto his back. I don't give him a chance to think before I straddle his hips, sinking down on his cock.

He grips my waist, his head falling back as I grind down on him. "Take it, baby. Show my dick who owns it."

Digging my nails into his chest, I roll my hips faster and faster until I'm bouncing up and down, riding us both into oblivion.

"Dex, I'm going to come again. Shit." I'm so fucking close, about to ride that wave again until he grabs me by the throat, pulling me down on top of him.

"Not yet." He growls before crushing his lips to mine, flipping me onto my back once again.

He ravages my mouth, stealing the breath from my lungs and I sink into the abyss with him. It's harsh, painful, and fucking delicious. The primal need between us is raw and uncontrollable.

He rises to his knees, the hand around my throat tightening. My eyes widen, fear tickling my senses as it becomes harder to breathe.

He smirks. "Surprise, baby. You're about to have the most intense orgasm of your fucking life."

He slams into me over and over, his hand squeezing tighter. My inner walls clench around him, arousal gushing from my pussy. My vision darkens at the corners, my breaths coming in short pants. I've never felt anything like this and I'm pretty sure this will be my new addiction.

"You want my cum, wife?" He taunts.

His big cock hammers inside me to the point its almost painful and the lack of oxygen has me on the verge of passing out. I nod the best I can, desperately wanting him to fill me with his cum.

My mouth opens with a silent scream as my body explodes, little bursts of light dancing across my eyes.

He releases my throat and I gasp for air, but the combination of his brutal cock and excess oxygen has my body arching off the ground, a hoarse scream piercing the night air.

Two more deep thrusts and he falls on top of me, burying his face in my neck while he empties himself inside of me. His deep groans and hot cum are enough to make me come again.

He moves in and out of me slowly, dragging out our orgasms until we're both spent.

After a few moments of trying to catch our breath, he raises his head, his eyes meeting mine. "That's the best anniversary present you could've given me."

Cupping his cheek, I smile. "Same."

He chuckles before kissing me softly, a contradiction to what just happened between us.

"You're everything to me, Savannah." He whispers against my lips, gazing into my eyes. "I never expected to find the love of my life when I moved into that shitty apartment building to protect a young, traumatized girl from her sadistic uncle. But here we are. You're the reason I breathe, little chaos. The reason I wake up every day. You are the reason for my existence. I was put on this earth to love you. Until my dying breath, I will love you and protect you with everything I am."

Tears burn the back of my eyes. "Same." I croak.

He grins, leaning down to kiss me again. It's slow and passionate and lets me feel all the love between us. As we lie in the dirt, in the middle of the woods across the way from our cute little cabin, I know I'd do anything for my husband.

I'll live for him.

I'll die for him.

I'll love him with everything I have until I leave this world.

Even then, I'll wait for him on the other side.

He watches me, his eyes soft as if he can read my thoughts. I may not be as poetic, but he knows how I feel about him. I don't have to describe it or try to put it into words.

He knew he had me before I did and that alone tells him all he needs to know.

I'm his.

He's mine.

"I love you, Archer."

His fingers trail down my side, stopping at the chaos symbol he loves to draw circles around. "I love you, little chaos."

Acknowledgement

I would like to thank my amazing beta readers. Katelin, Amber, Stacy and Kenzie. You four ladies mean the world to me and I'm lucky to have you on this wild journey. Your input is valued and taken to heart, always.

To my ARC readers, you are wild and beautiful. You all made me laugh in our ARC chat and I will think of you everytime I see the "leg" emoji. It is permanently imprinted in my mind.

To my readers, without you, my stories would only be my own. As an Indie Author, I have unlimited blank pages to create my own little world with characters I love. Without your support and encouragement, they would never see the light of day. You all mean so much to me and I'm forever grateful for your kind words and love of my stories.

To my husband, I love you.

Books By This Author

Reaper

Trauma changes a person.
When I met the devil at eight years old, it changed
the course of my life.
Lost and alone, anger controlled my every
thought.
Happiness was out of reach until the day I found
my calling.

At sixteen years old, they never saw me coming.
As an adult, I'm the Reaper they fear.
Seeking vengeance for all the victims who were
silenced.

Darkness ruled my world until I laid eyes on her.
A sliver of light trickled into my life, and I would
do anything to hold onto it.
I stole her heart.
I own her soul.
She's my wife.
The one person I'd give my life to protect at any
cost.

She thinks she knows all my secrets.

The man she loves is a serial killer and she doesn't have a clue.
Or does she?
It seems she has a secret of her own.
When lies are exposed and the truth is revealed, our lives will change forever.

Rage

All I've ever known is violence.
After being abused by the people closest to me, I despise being touched.
Many nights of my past were spent wishing for death.

The time came when I'd had enough.
I snapped, taking back my life while ending another.
Things took a turn for the better, but defending myself never changed.
The night a stranger put his hands on me in the park, my blade came out to play.

I wasn't counting on the gorgeous stranger witnessing my wrath.
I didn't expect him to watch me from the shadows every night after.

I want to hate him, but his dark eyes and deadly

past have me intrigued.
No matter how much I push him away, or want to kill him, I don't.

His filthy words unravel me.
His touch sets me on fire.

As darkness collides, obsession turns into something deeper.

He knows my secrets.
He's earned my trust.
He owns my body.
Giving him my heart?
It may get us both killed...

His Good Girl

For two years, I've been content alone. Being married to a narcissist did me in. I'm a book editor who works from home and I'm okay with that.

Until the gorgeous man covered in tattoos notices me. Suddenly, I don't want to be alone anymore.

It starts out as a story book romance, but much dirtier.
A second chance at finding love.

But our pasts have other plans, and they collide in a way we never could have imagined...

Entwined

Three chance encounters...

Shelby Carter is making the move to Emerald Hills to start a new life with her best friend, Ava.
Meeting her motorcycle riding landlord, she falls hard for the sexy stranger.
Damien McCallister is content living in the mountains, running a cabin rental business.
Everything changes when he meets his new tenant. He realizes he's been missing something.
Their chemistry is explosive.
The stars align as their souls entwine.

Ava Larson is excited to have her best friend close again.
When she meets Shelby and Damien for dinner one night, she doesn't expect to meet the man of her dreams.
Chase Brooks loves his peaceful life in Emerald Hills. He has everything he needs.
Or so he thought.
One look at Ava and his world is changed forever. He will do everything in his power to capture her heart.

Lucas Campbell is a grump. He moved to Emerald Hills after retiring from his job as a bouncer in Atlanta.

He's doesn't like people, so when he feels the pull to visit the local bar one night, he's baffled.

Until he sees her...

Scarlett Ellis is trying to ignore the guy flirting with her at the bar. She's all but given up on finding love until her eyes lock with a giant who steals her breath.

He's the sexiest man she's ever seen, and she knows her fate is sealed.

The Emerald Hills Series includes three novellas, each with a guaranteed HEA.

Souls Entwined
Hearts Entwined
Passions Entwined

If you love short, fast-paced, insta-love books with extra spice and a happy ending, this is the series for you.

This is the author's debut series.

Made in the USA
Columbia, SC
26 May 2025

58389092R00146